WILD GEESE
and
TEA

SHU SHU COSTA

Riverhead Books

New York

1997

WILD GEESE

and

TEA

An   Asian – American

Wedding   Planner

Riverhead Books
a division of G. P. Putnam's Sons
Publishers Since 1838
200 Madison Avenue
New York, New York 10016

Library of Congress Cataloging-in-Publication Data

Costa, Shu Shu, date.
  Wild geese and tea :
  an Asian–American wedding planner /
  Shu Shu Costa
    p.   cm.
  Includes index.
  ISBN 1-57322-040-X (alk. paper)
  1. Weddings—United States—Planning.
  2. Asian Americans—Marriage.
  I. Title.
  HQ745.C67   1997   96-28421 CIP
  395′.22′08995073—dc20

Printed in the United States of America
10   9   8   7   6   5   4   3   2   1

Book design by Judith Stagnitto Abbate

This book is printed on acid-free paper. ⊗

Acknowledgments

I AM GRATEFUL to the many people who offered encouragement, enthusiasm, and support for this book. In the course of writing it, I have learned how vibrant, warm, and cohesive the Asian-American community is, and what a growing sense of self it has. The many friends I've made along the way have nurtured my own sense of being Asian-American, bringing to life a part of me that surprises me with its comfort and familiarity. For that, and so much more, I thank them.

Special thanks go to the experts in all fields who have given of their time, their knowledge, and their hearts to this project; to my editors at Putnam, Julie Grau and Nicole Wan, who have become true friends; to my agents, Barbara Lowenstein and Madeleine Morel, for their encouragement; to my copy editor, Anna Jardine, for her meticulous care; and to Millie Martini Bratten, editor at *Bride's,* for her confidence. I also thank my friends who have bolstered me with their unceasing excitement about the book, cheerful advice, and great love.

My deepest thanks go to my family. My parents, Hong and Sally Foo, who, through their wonderful example, taught me about love, and who have been the strongest pillars in my life; my brother, Kean, who is a great friend; my husband's family, his sisters Kim Barré and Stephanie Brand, and especially my in-laws Keith and Beverly Costa, who always offer unlimited love and support—often in the form of late-night calls; and most of all my son, Keith Yeh, who has been more patient and giving than a toddler knows.

Finally, thanks to Christopher, my best friend, my best editor, my biggest fan, my husband.

To my love, Christopher

Contents

THE TEA WAS SIMPLE and sweet, created by boiling dried "dragon's eye" fruit in water. It was offered by me and my new husband, with small, humble bows, to the relatives seated before us, one by one. A dainty sip was all that was required, and the teacup was given back with a little red envelope, or *hung bao,* filled with money or jewelry. With this traditional tea ceremony, witnessed by our ancestors as well as the gods above, we were formally introduced to our families as husband and wife.

Like many couples from different heritages, my husband and I borrowed from our separate cultures to make the wedding our own. Our planning was inspired by more than just a desire to be different: it was as though we had gathered what made us unique and offered it to our families, our guests, and each other, saying, "See who we are. See who we can become." The offering of tea was the third event of that hot Long Island August day—our guests had already witnessed two religious ceremonies. Each rite, each detail of the day, was one more silken tie that bound us together. Now our two families were forever joined, as we collected around the dance floor of the ornate Chinese restaurant, and laughed at the traditional fertility jokes made by my gregarious uncle and smiled when my mother, her eyes a bit too shiny, proclaimed the tea the sweetest she'd ever had.

After the intimate ceremony came the great feast. No Asian festivity is complete without a grand banquet; food is central to every celebration. Trays of mouth-watering dishes streamed endlessly from the kitchen: spicy chicken, succulent pig, delicate seafood, long, long noodles, the symbol of long life—twelve courses in all. Finally the wedding cake appeared, shaped like a Chinese pagoda but decorated with an English garden of pastel flowers and birds. As the guests mingled under the red silk banner with the double characters of happiness, lilies scenting the room with their delicate perfume, the wild geese outside contentedly nestled beneath tree boughs. I like to think that the presence of these birds, the traditional symbol of marital harmony, was a nod of approval from the gods.

A wedding, after all, is about tradition and roots and family. It is an event steeped in symbolism, when two lives, two worlds, and often two cultures are joined as one. For Asian-Americans, tokens of home and tradition represent continuity with family far away, and show honor and respect for ancient heritage. A Japanese-American couple, for example, may serve their guests the traditional dish of sea bream—whose Japanese name, *tai*, recalls the word for "lucky." A Korean-American bride may choose to wear the bright red and yellow silk wedding dress of her grandmother and a beaded cap. A Chinese-American groom may offer his new wife a tangerine, representing good fortune, and their wedding guests may bring pictures of wild geese to the ceremony. Like the scattering of rice or the tossing of the bouquet, these details have meanings deeper than they appear, touching hearts and linking generations in this romantic ritual.

This book is about such traditions. Today, more than ever, modern couples are seeking ways to make their weddings more meaningful, more unique. As Asians marry Westerners or other Asians with different upbringings, the traditional white Victorian wedding is being transformed into a dazzling display of ethnic color and culture. For couples transplanted far from their roots, separated from village elders and grandparents, this book will bring to life some of the mystery and fascination of the rich and colorful history of the Chinese, Japanese, and Korean traditions. It will explore the meanings behind the rituals and rites that are so important during this life passage. The Chinese believe that all marriages are guided by the twin gods of mirth and harmony. Together, they symbolize the very essence of this wedding book—"two in body, one in spirit."

PART I

Of Spirits and Heartstrings

Chapter One

A MARRIAGE MADE
IN HEAVEN

The outside grandparents had four daughters, and so one of this grandmother's habits whenever she heard of an interesting boy or young man was to count him. Using the poor people's divining method, she took a pinchful of rice, said his name, and counted the grains to see if she had picked an odd or even number, carefully dropping each speck back into the rice box. Odd meant Yes, this boy was her daughter's true husband; even meant No, wrong boy; four sounds like die. In addition to counting rice, she confirmed the results by paying an expensive blind fortuneteller to touch a list of young men's names, and he picked out her future son-in-law. He also used the yarrow sticks and tortoise shell and told the wedding date.

—MAXINE HONG KINGSTON,
CHINA MEN

THE ANCIENT ASIANS believed in destiny. They lived in a world full of happy-go-lucky gods who sat around the kitchen, ancestors who loomed in the

The Legend of the Weaving Maiden and Her Cowherd

In ancient Asia, on the seventh day of the seventh month, girls prayed to the Weaving Maiden, patroness of unmarried women, asking her to find them good husbands. The day is still special in Japan, as it is the time for the annual tryst between this beautiful goddess and her husband and true love, the cowherd.

The tale goes like this: The Emperor of Heaven's seven daughters descended to earth one day to bathe in a river near a green meadow. One of them, the Weaving Maiden, was very skilled in weaving. A passing cowherd became enamored of her beauty and stole her clothes, thereby preventing her from returning to her home in the heavens. When she discovered the thief, however, she fell deeply in love with him.

The two were soon married and lived happily for many years. They were so happy that the Weaving Maiden stopped her weaving and the cowherd stopped tending to his animals. The Queen Mother of the West became upset at this negligence and ordered the Weaving Maiden back to heaven. Obediently, she donned her old clothes and flew up to the sky. The cowherd tried to follow, but the Queen Mother took a golden hairpin from her head and drew a river of stars between them.

shadows, and mischievous evil spirits who lurked in the most unexpected places. These gods and spirits were not as untouchable as Western gods, but were rather of the next-door neighbor variety, ready to dip their hands into human affairs as they saw fit. Asian folklore has countless stories of their sometimes capricious ways, like that of the poor man who fell in love with a beautiful woman he met in a field, and married her only to realize that, in his whim, he had wed a ghost. In the minds of the ancients, the line between the world of spirits and the world of mortals was very thin. No wonder, then, that much time was spent divining the wishes of these powerful beings, who controlled everything from the season's harvest to one's life's partner.

Legend has it that, at birth, the gods tie an invisible red string around the ankles of a man and a woman destined to be husband and wife. As the years pass, the string grows shorter and shorter, until finally they are united. Nothing can break the string, not distance, not changing circumstances, not even love. Destiny always has its day. The red string appears in a Chinese T'ang dynasty folktale in which an up-and-coming official named Wei Ku meets an old gentleman reading a scroll by the light of the moon, a mysterious red string in a bag at his feet.

"Strange," says Wei Ku to the old man, "I can read many scripts but cannot decipher yours."

"Of course not," the old man answers laughing. "This document is not from this world."

The old man, actually a god, is reviewing his list of future husbands and wives. Wei Ku, an orphan who has searched ten years for a bride of his own, asks the man his fate. He is told he will marry the vegetable seller's daughter, who will one day give birth to a famous son. Much relieved, Wei Ku walks with the old man across town to sneak a glimpse of the child who will one day be Wei Ku's bride.

But when he sees her poor upbringing, he is aghast. Determined to change his destiny, Wei Ku asks the old man, "If I kill her, will I be given another wife?"

"No," the man replies, "she is not to die. Once the red string is tied, it can never be untied."

After the old man disappears, Wei Ku sends his servant to kill the girl. The servant stabs her in the head and flees.

Years later, now an important official, Wei Ku marries the niece of his superior officer. When they are alone in their chamber after the wedding ceremony, he lifts her heavy veil to look at her face for the first time. To his great surprise, there is a scar above her eyebrow. The red string tied their fates together after all.

On a clear night, you can see the Weaving Maiden and her beloved in the night sky. She is the star Vega in the constellation Lyra, and he is the constellation Aquila. On most nights, they are separated by that great river the Milky Way. But for one night a year, the seventh night of the seventh month, the two are allowed to unite once more. Flocks of magpies form a fragile bridge for the Weaving Maiden to cross. If it rains on that day, it is the two star-crossed lovers shedding tears of sadness, yearning for the next time they will meet.

The Village Matchmaker

Gods and fate aside, most people in Asia had little to say about whom they would marry anyway. Marriage was for continuing the ancestral line and creating alliances between families—too important a duty to be left in the rash hands of the young. Partners were chosen by the parents with the assistance of matchmakers, semi-professional gossips who went from village to village proclaiming the sterling qualities of some local man or woman. If a family was interested, the matchmaker would set up a meeting of the two parties.

In Chinese villages today, matchmakers still host betrothal teas, where nervous partners get their first glimpses of each other. At this meeting, the prospective bride serves tea to the potential groom and his family. If he approves of her, he places an embroidered red bag on his saucer. If she agrees, she accepts the pouch. But if she disapproves of him, she leaves the room before the pouch is even offered. In most villages of old Asia, however, bride and groom never saw each other before the wedding day and had no say in the decision. And love? Love was allowed, even glorified in some cases—but it had no part to play in proper marriage.

In olden times, a potential mate sent each side's parents hurrying to the gods and the ancestors for approval. Was this the true red string? Many people, like the old grandmother who counted rice grains in Maxine Hong Kingston's *China Men,* had their own methods of divining the wishes of the gods. General Tou Yi of China's Sui dynasty devised a test of skill for his daughter's prospective mate. An amateur astrologer, the general was convinced his daughter would marry a future emperor. He set up a screen with a peacock painting in his main hall. Suitors were asked to shoot two arrows at the screen. Secretly, the general told himself that the one who hit both the peacock's eyes would marry the general's daughter.

Months passed, with many suitors but none successful. One

day a young officer named Li Yuan tried his hand. To the general's delight, he pierced the peacock's eyes precisely and won the young woman's hand. And as predicted, Li Yuan became emperor, the first of the T'ang dynasty.

Most prospective male suitors were not subject to such rigorous tests of skill. It was more likely for the couple's "eight characters" (Chinese) or "four pillars" (Korean)—the year, month, day, and hour of birth—to be exchanged. These vital statistics were supposed to predict a person's fate. The local fortune-teller was summoned to determine whether the couple could live together harmoniously, in a process the Koreans call *kung-hap*. The approval of the fortune-teller was important. As an old Korean saying goes: "Straw sandals are useful only when they fit your feet."

The Fortune-Teller's Secrets

While there may have been fortune-tellers with supernatural powers, some of their tests of compatibility were simple. First, they compared the couple's surnames. Confucius ruled that people with the same last name could not marry; the rule is still enforced in many places in Asia. In fact, South Korea set aside the rule only as late as 1995, thereby increasing the pool of potential mates—in a country where one out of

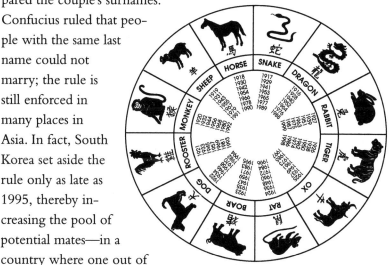

THE HERD BOY AND THE MAIDEN

Distant and faint the Herd-Boy Star,
Bright and lustrous the Heavenly River Maid;
Gently plying her slender white hands,
Cha-cha hum her shuttle and loom.
Day after day, her pattern unfinished,
Her tears fall in droplets like rain.
The Heavenly River, shallow and clear,
Divides them now by only a space;
Lovely and tender, with the river between,
Longingly, they look but cannot speak.

—Anonymous Chinese poet, fifth or sixth century A.D.

every five people is named Lee—by about twenty-five percent. (South Koreans with the same last name must be married outside the country, though.)

It was also important that the man's name dominate the woman's. If, for example, the man's name contained the character for "water" and the woman's name meant "fire," peace would reign in the household, for water can quench fire. But woe betide the marriage of this fiery woman with a man of the name "wood"!

Modern prognosticators also use astrology to gauge the gods' advice. The ancient Asian zodiac is separated into a cycle of twelve years, each bearing the name and traits of an animal: rat, ox, tiger, rabbit, dragon, snake, horse, sheep, monkey, rooster, dog, and boar. It is believed the most contentious marriages are those between spouses born in years of animals opposite each other on the astro-logical compass. The power-hungry dragon and the proud dog, for instance, would not live well together, nor would the steadfast ox and the free-spirited sheep.

Fortune-tellers approve of marriages between those people whose year signs suggest compatibility. People born in the years of the rat, the dragon, and the monkey are ambitious and strong-minded, and would therefore make a strong match. (My parents, married thirty years, are a dragon–monkey couple.) The ox, the snake, and the rooster are steady and trustworthy. The tiger, the horse, and the dog share idealistic, humanitarian values. And the rab-bit, the sheep, and the boar tend to be emotional and artistic.

But while the word of the soothsayer was taken as a sign from the gods, in truth few people turned away potential mates. Breaking up an intended marriage was considered unlucky.

In China, if the stars were favorable, the prospective groom's family wrote the bride's "eight characters" on a sheet of rice paper and placed it on the family ancestral altar, a small mantel for incense and offerings in honor of the ancestors. If nothing disastrous hap-pened in three days—an illness in the family, a broken vase or dish— the marriage was deemed approved. The process was repeated by the

This gourd-shaped pitcher from Korea's Koryo dynasty dates back to the late eleventh or early twelfth century. As a traditional wedding vow, bride and groom sipped wine from two halves of a gourd grown by the bride's mother. Etched onto this pitcher's surface are a pair of mandarin ducks and a pair of wild geese, symbols of marital harmony.

bride's family, with the groom's "eight characters." If all went well, the couple's characters were recorded on the same piece of red paper— a symbolic marriage contract. The paper, decorated with auspicious couplets and verse, was then presented to the bride's family, and the festivities began.

Today, in local Chinatowns and Little Koreas, fortune-tellers can still be found to read your fate. And many couples, some for fun, some to please an anxious parent, do give in to the lure of the gods.

On the morning of his wedding, the Korean groom presents a wooden duck, or kirogi, to his future mother-in-law as a sign of his faithfulness to her daughter. The custom originated with a live wild goose, an animal that mates for life; wooden ducks were substituted when live geese became hard to obtain. The bride's mother would feed noodles to the goose as a sign of her approval. Thus "feeding noodles to a goose" became an expression for marriage. These days, when people ask an unmarried woman, "When are you going to have us over for noodles?" they mean, "When are you going to get married?"

One American groom even proposed to his Chinese-American wife on an auspicious day to satisfy her tradition-inclined mother. Asian wedding planners juggling calendars know enough to ask whether a ceremony date was picked by the couple or fixed by the stars. For Korean-Americans, exchanging the "four pillars" has evolved into another tradition. At the family engagement party, the parents formally exchange slips of handmade rice paper with the bride's and groom's information written in calligraphy—a bow to the gods above.

Modern Matches

Matchmakers, too, have come into modern times. While arranged marriages are frowned on in the West, in Japan many marriages start off with a little help from a local Cupid. Common from samurai

THE MODERN MATCHMAKER

Matchmakers have been around in Japan since the seventeenth century, but it wasn't until about a hundred years ago that a creative man in Osaka hung out the first matchmaker's shingle, a sign announcing, in Japanese, INTRODUCTIONS FOR MARRIAGE. Since then, matchmaking has become an industry, with technology playing a big role. One computer dating service, or *kekkon sodanjo*, programs as many as 1,271 facts about each of its clients, from their financial status to their favorite ice cream flavor. Such services even use digital imaging telephones to introduce prospective mates who live far away from each other. Magazines devoted to the concerns of these singles seeking singles, and *miai* parties round out the modern matchmaking industry. Don't laugh: One computer dating firm in Tokyo claims to have matched at least 17,600 people in the last seven years. And to its knowledge, only three couples have filed for divorce.

If you're thinking of going into business yourself, remember this: There are great responsibilities to being a go-between, or *nakodo*. *Nakodo* lend their good name and own success at marriage to the wedding. They make the first speech at the ceremony, sit at a place of high honor at the reception, and receive a gift equal to $1,000 to $2,000 for their troubles. As guarantors of the match, they are responsible for a couple's happiness their entire lives, and act as mediators should problems arise. Before a couple file for divorce, they are obliged to consult with their *nakodo* first.

The Toad Bridegroom

Here's a Korean fairy tale that tells of the rewards of arranged marriages. The moral: Obey your parents.

A large toad wished to marry one of three sisters. Their father approached each of his daughters, and the first two turned away in disgust. The youngest, however, cheerfully agreed, and was married at once. People came from far and near to witness this bizarre wedding. The two older daughters sneered at their sister's new husband, but she ignored them with a smile.

When the toad and his bride were alone on their wedding night, he voiced a strange request. He asked her to cut open his skin with scissors. Alarmed, she at first refused, but he gently insisted. The toad skin shed, out stepped a handsome man, a young god. The toad bridegroom took her arm and winged them up to heaven, where he and his bride lived happily ever after.

times to before World War II, arranged, or *miai,* marriages were once a way to maintain or advance the status of the family and thus were the complete domain of the parents. Even as late as the 1950s, family interests were so important many parents hired detectives to investigate a potential spouse's background.

These days, parental control has loosened a bit. A modern matchmaker may be a family friend, an aunt, a boss, or even a computer system that acts as a personal dating service. To make the job easier, young people in Japan put together personal résumés for distribution to potential matches, containing a brief description of their occupation, education, and family background, and the all-important photograph. And although most modern *miai* marriages begin with an introduction, the couple are free to date and choose as they wish. To be sure, *ren-ai,* or marrying for love, is now more common in Japan than *miai.* But the tradition continues: about a third of all marriages are arranged.

Here in the West, most people marry for love. But for many Asian-Americans who meet and choose to marry as they wish, the voice of the family—perhaps it is the echo of the ancestors?—whispers loudly. Family has always been paramount in communal Asian societies, overshadowing and overpowering the meek individual. The Chinese word for marriage, *hun-yin,* implies not just a joining of individuals, but a relationship between families. The ties are spiritual as well as physical, memories and emotion running as deep as blood. For first-generation Asians, ancestral bonds may be reflected in a parent who speaks no English, only the language of his or her village, who prefers soba to sirloin, who remembers the old ways. Even as memories fade for the following generations, the whispers remain—in a grandmother's kimono, in the desire to preserve ancient traditions and ceremonies that may seem to hold little meaning in your modern life, but which shine strangely bright on your inner family altar.

Those ancient ceremonies hold a special power, their meaning timeless and life-affirming. Marriage is an ancient rite, but the weaving of family, ritual, legends, and gods creates a foundation for couples to build a life on today. In Korea, couples drink wine poured from a pitcher into two halves of a gourd grown by the bride's mother. A gift of a wild duck from the groom to the bride's mother seals his promise to care for her daughter forever. Unspoken, yet not unheard, are the powerful meanings these simple gestures convey, the basis for true, lasting bonds: love, honor, respect, fidelity, unity. These and other traditions remind you that no matter how different your lives might seem from lives in the days of old, the same truths hold.

So as you wear the silk dress of your ancestors, or bow in respect to your new family, or sip wine with your new spouse, take a moment to listen to the footsteps of your ancestors. Together, you and your partner will create your own traditions. But today, as you stand, breathless and joyful, at this glorious spot between your past and your future, believe and treasure, with all your heart, the power of that little red string.

Chapter Two

RINGS, SEAWEED, AND RIPENED MILLET: THE BETROTHAL

When I first met my lady
I stood like a wallflower

Now, love is budding in me
Like blooming spring flower

When will this love bear fruit to make
Me feel tall like a sunflower?

—KIM WOOKYU (B. 1661),
KOREAN POET AND MUSICIAN

FOR OUR ANCESTORS, an engagement was a promise, a promise almost as binding as the wedding itself. After the exchange of an astounding array of gifts—the finest fabrics, symbolic foods, generous amounts of money—the engaged couple was as good as married. In Sung dynasty China, the two families began referring to

Come make one heart
add mine to yours
Or if you love me
take my heart!

Come make one heart
share more than tears
add mine if not
leave yours with me.

Come make one heart
again if not
return my heart
but add your tears   .
so I may weep
with all my heart
for two
singly.

Then if my heart
returns to me
with added tears
lover I might
love even tears
like constancy.

—Han Yong-Woon, from
  Meditations of the Lover

A Buddhist poet and scholar,
Han Yong-Woon (1879–1944)
was one of the famed Thirty-three,
the signers of the Korean declara-
tion of independence from Japan.

each other as relatives after the betrothal. And in the courts of law, breaking an engagement was a fate punishable by "sixty strokes" (with what, we dare not ask). Engagements made when people were young children—some were promised to each other as infants, or even when still in the womb—could be broken only if, by the time of the marriage, "one or the other turns out to be unworthy or unreliable or develops a loathsome disease."

The proposal itself was probably not romantic. In China, a formal letter of betrothal was sent from the groom's father or grandfather to the bride's father, asking for her hand and listing the many gifts the groom's family could offer, a fancy, dressed-up "bride price," or payment for the bride. In Japan and Korea, a go-between might make the first move, followed by a representative from each of the families. It was considered inappropriate for the groom to ask the woman or her family himself—this might seem a relief for today's men! As late as 1972, a Japanese suitor who approached his intended's parents alone was turned away at the door, and told to bring a member of the older generation.

When the proposal was finally accepted, the arrangement was sealed with gifts—mostly from the groom's family to the bride's. And not just any gifts, but the finest the family could afford. There were meanings hidden in the many offerings, which often symbolized traditional wishes for children, longevity, and happiness. Because marriage was a linking of families, the gifts also carried with them bonds of obligation and mutual responsibility.

As you find ways to celebrate your happiness, you may want to turn to the betrothal customs and gift-giving traditions of your past. Rituals varied from region to region, village to village: your family's practice may vary from the descriptions here. Follow the rituals completely, or choose only what strikes your heart.

Fish are significant in Asian wedding rituals. For both the Chinese and the Koreans, they symbolize abundance and wealth. (The Chinese word for "fish," yu, also sounds like the word for "plenty.") Live fish and jewelry in the shape of fish were traditional gifts for Chinese brides, and whole fish is still an important part of a wedding banquet. At Japanese wedding banquets, sea bream is served as a wish for good fortune. The term for it in Japanese, tai, is part of the word for "lucky," omedetai.

Chinese: Twelve Gifts

The ancient marriage ritual guide, *The Book of Rites,* based on the teachings of Confucius, enumerates six betrothal ceremonies.

After a letter of betrothal from the groom's father was received and accepted by the bride's father, the gifts to her family began arriving—the first ceremony. In Taiwan, the groom would give the bride twelve gifts. In the countryside, these might be live animals, always given in pairs to symbolize marriage. For city dwellers, shoes, clothing, bolts of silk cloth, and gold jewelry might be given, along with such foods as sugar-coated winter melon, dried *longan* (the "dragon's eye" fruit), pagoda-shaped candies, and a whole roast pig. With the gifts came a substantial sum of money as payment for the bride. Some families might spend half their annual income on a bride; twenty or thirty years ago in Taiwan, the average sum would be close to $2,500. As the gifts arrived, the letter of betrothal was read to the bride's family—the second ceremony.

In reply to the groom's largesse, the bride's family would politely return a portion of the gifts (roosters, for example, were always returned to ensure the good luck of the groom's family) and offer twelve more of their own. This showed the generosity of the bride's family and subtly implied that they were wealthy enough to return the gifts. A pair of wine jars, each filled with fresh water and four goldfish, and a pair of chopsticks and two onions might be offered. These gifts were rich in symbolism: the word for "fish," *yu,* sounds like the word for "plenty": a wish for abundance and wealth for the couple. The word for "chopsticks," *fai ji,* sounds like "fast boy": a wish for sons— soon. In the Sung dynasty capital of Hangchow, the richer families gave fish and chopsticks made of gold, and onions made of silk.

Other symbolic gifts included deer horn, a Chinese medicine as well as an aphrodisiac, and sweet osmanthus and pomegranate flowers, which symbolize prosperity and many sons. Tea, in ancient times a most expensive and precious gift, was presented by the groom's family to the bride. Her acceptance meant that she was officially engaged. (The word *chali,* or "tea gift," has become the term for "engagement.") The bride's family returned the head and the hind portion of the roast pig, thus showing that to everything in life, there was a beginning and an end. The family also sent along the bride's lineage, the names of her father, grandfather, and great-grandfather, to complete the third ceremony.

Later—in the fourth ceremony—the groom's family sent a marriage contract with the couple's "eight characters" and auspicious verse. The wedding date was then set, in the fifth ceremony. The sixth and final ceremony was the wedding itself.

Chinese-Americans keep these traditions alive today by holding large engagement parties, with lots of family and food. Start

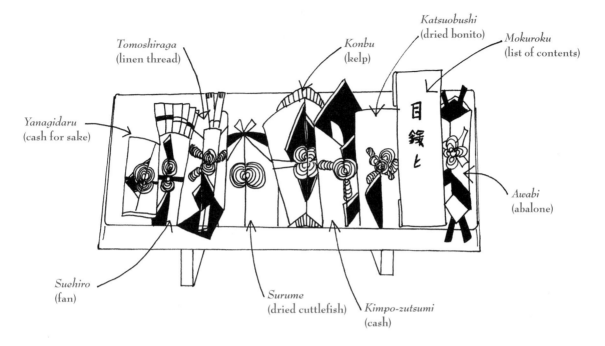

Yanagidaru
(cash for sake)

Tomoshiraga
(linen thread)

Konbu
(kelp)

Katsuobushi
(dried bonito)

Mokuroku
(list of contents)

目録ト

Awabi
(abalone)

Suehiro
(fan)

Surume
(dried cuttlefish)

Kimpo-zutsumi
(cash)

your festivities off by inviting your new family over to celebrate and exchange gifts, perhaps even traditional ones. One Western groom surprised his fiancée's mother with a whole roast pig, trucked up from New York City to Boston. Mercifully for him, she didn't offer him the head and hind in return.

Japanese: The *Yuino*

In old Japan also, the engagement was sealed by the offering of gifts. In a ceremony called the *yuino,* the go-between, or *nakodo,* would deliver the presents from the groom's family to the bride's. After eating a little feast, the *nakodo* was given a receipt for the gifts, which he brought back to the groom's family. The groom's family gave him more food, drink, and a small cash gift for his trouble.

Today, the *yuino* is more often held at the woman's home, with the future bride and groom, their parents, and the *nakodo* pres-

At the engagement ceremony, or yuino, the Japanese groom offers these symbolic items to his bride-to-be and her family. The linen thread represents the white hair of a couple married many years; the phallic-shaped cuttlefish is a wish for many children; and seaweed is included because the Japanese term, konbu, can also mean "child-bearing woman."

You can share your good news with friends near and far by announcing your engagement in a local Asian-American paper. The announcement is made in the name of the bride's parents, even when the article is published in the groom's hometown. An announcement is sent to a paper two or three months before the wedding.

Call the paper and ask for the editor in charge of engagement and wedding announcements. Don't send an engraved or printed announcement; the paper may have a special form to fill out or may suggest a format. Type, double-spaced, all information you give the newspaper. Include an address and a telephone number where you can be contacted to verify any information. A photograph, of the bride or the couple, may be submitted.

Here is a sample basic announcement, adapted from guidelines of the Association of Bridal Consultants:

Mr. and Mrs. Henry Teoh of Austin, Texas, announce the engagement of their daughter Miss Melissa Teoh to Mr. Steven Ng, son of Dr. and Mrs. Paul Ng of Lima, Ohio. A July wedding is planned.

Miss Teoh graduated from Rice University and is an engineer with DigiCorp in New York City. Mr. Ng graduated from Duke University and is a student at Yale Law School.

ent. As in olden days, cloth or clothing, and food and drink are given by the groom and his family, along with symbolic offerings such as dried cuttlefish in a phallic shape, a pair of fish, male and female, placed belly to belly, and a piece of seaweed called *konbu*—the character for *konbu* can be written to mean "child-bearing woman," and the sound of the word calls to mind the last half of *yorokobu,* joy. Other gifts convey the wish for a long married life: a long linen thread or hempen cord, which represents the couple's hair grown white with age, and a folding fan, which spreads out wide to show future wealth and future growth in numbers. The gifts are wrapped in ornate rice-paper envelopes made for formal occasions.

The main gift from the groom's family to the bride's was, and still is, money, tucked into a *shugi-bukuro,* a special envelope, tied with gold and silver strings which are impossible to unknot. There is also cash for sake, cash for wedding clothes, and just plain cash. The rule of thumb of how much to give is usually determined by three months of the groom's salary, or the fixed amount of 500,000 yen (roughly $5,000). Expensive? Don't worry: most grooms don't amass this money themselves. The gift is seen as a family-to-family payment, and is left to the parents to provide.

After the gifts are presented on a tray, the bride's father presents the groom's family with a formal, symbolic receipt; then the two families share a meal. These days, Japanese wedding halls offer to conduct the *yuino,* providing a master of ceremonies to help with the protocol, a supply of traditional gifts, and of course, the food. You may wish to hold your own *yuino,* or host an intimate dinner with both sets of parents.

Korean: Buy a *Hahm!*

In Korea too, the betrothal is a time for family get-togethers, convened in the family home of the bride. Traditionally, family members would sit around a long table with the couple at the head and the parents at their sides. Each family member would be formally introduced, and then the meal would be served.

Gifts from the groom's family would be delivered on the eve of the wedding day. With blackened faces and costumes—some would sport a mask of dried squid!—a group of the groom's friends, dancing to drumbeats, would carry a large box, or *hahm,* containing gifts for the bride: stalks of ripened millet, a wish for many children; silk cloth for the wedding dress; gold jewelry. The friends would pause near the bride's home, chanting, *"Hahm* for sale, buy a *hahm,"* as her family rushed out to greet the procession. With laughter and teasing, the gift bearers would demand money for each step forward. Bit by bit, coin by coin, the group would be lured in, until, finally, they relinquished their box of treasures. After accepting the family's offer of food and drink, they would be on their way.

Korean-Americans have adapted these traditions into their engagement ceremonies. Formal introductions remain a must, but the families are as likely to meet at a local Korean restaurant as at the woman's home. The bride wears a special engagement dress, or *hanbok,* colored a delicate or a bright pink. Entertainment is also expected. Families might hire a traditional Korean harpist to play the *kayakum.* Family members might be prodded to offer a song to the couple, either with accompaniment in the form of a hired karaoke machine or a cappella.

Gifts are also exchanged. One Korean-American bride was given enough jewelry to fill a small safe. In return, her family provided "ritual silk," buying the wedding outfits of all the members of the groom's family. Some Korean-American families spend $30,000 to $40,000 on engagement gifts alone. Each gift has a special meaning. The same Korean-American woman's father gave the groom-to-be a Rolex watch: a symbol of the quality time the couple would spend together.

Family crests, or mon, *were given to the samurai class. A man always takes his father's crest, while a woman takes her mother's. If you don't know your family's* mon, *a little research may prove fruitful: check for crests on family gravestones or on kimonos in old family photographs. A few books, such as* The Elements of Japanese Design *by John W. Dower and* Japanese Crest Designs *by W. M. Hawley, give family crests.*

Jeweled Traditions

While many Asian-Americans follow their culture's gift-giving traditions, most men also give their fiancées engagement rings, or betrothal rings, as a sign of their love. The giving of rings, a Western tradition, has recently become popular in Asia as well—with some twists. (In Japan, sales of rings topped 197 billion yen—roughly $188 million—in 1993.) Honoring the Asian tradition of exchange, the women give gifts of their own, usually watches. The Taiwanese add more symbolism to the giving of rings. At the engagement banquet and tea ceremony traditionally held by the bride's family, bride and groom exchange gold rings in front of family and friends. The guests are sure to watch the couple carefully: the one to push his or her ring to the very base of the other's finger is seeking the upper hand in the marriage.

If you're looking for a ring with a more ethnic style, consider using different stones, such as ancient jade or the classic pearl, to enhance your diamond. For the Chinese, the silky-smooth jade, *yu,* is the jewel of heaven, the bridge between heaven and earth. Jade is given at all important life ceremonies, and it is considered good luck to own a piece, and even better luck to receive one. Jade, to the ancients, possessed magical qualities and was seen as the symbol of highest virtue. *The Book of Rites* says, "The superior man competes in virtue with jade." In *My Several Worlds,* Pearl S. Buck writes that "the poorest courtesan has her bit of jade . . . because jade is the most sumptuous jewel against a woman's flesh."

The warm, iridescent pearl is another classic wedding gem, prized in Asia, where so many pearls are harvested. Taoist mystics believed that the pearl was the essence of the moon and symbolized feminine beauty and purity. The ancient Greeks agreed, convinced that pearls promoted marital bliss and, oddly enough, stopped newlywed women from crying.

You might also design your own rings, with a Japanese family crest, for example, or a traditional motif such as a phoenix, the Chinese symbol of woman and queen. Contemporary Japanese-American jewelry designer Takashi Wada shapes metal to be so smooth it is soft to the touch, the tranquil lines reminiscent of a Zen garden. Among his creations, commissioned by a couple for their wedding, were double rings of silver and gold.

Sharing the Good News

In China, families first reported a betrothal to the ancestors by offering incense, candles, wine, and fruit on the ancestral altars. Similarly, let your families share your good news first. While it is no longer mandatory for a man to ask his fiancée's father for her hand, his discussing his intentions with her family shows courtesy and respect—especially for Asian families.

By Western custom, the families should meet as soon as possible after the proposal. The groom's parents should make the first contact, but the bride's parents can also offer an invitation. In old Korea, the bride would go to meet her in-laws first with one family member, usually not her parents. The intention was clear: The bride left her family behind to join another, never to return except on rare occasions. These days, though, weddings are a time to unite families. Long ago in China, brides would make soup with the heart of a pig for their in-laws, to show that they were all of one heart. A happy, celebratory first meeting—perhaps with more palatable fare—can likewise set the stage for smooth waters ahead.

After your parents have been told the good news, you are free to spread the word to other family members and friends. In China, the groom's family provided special cakes for the bride's family to distribute to relatives and friends, a sweet announcement of sorts. The cakes, some with a thin layer of syrup and topped with sesame seeds, would be given in large round lacquered boxes with the "double happiness" character inscribed in gold. In some villages,

Benten, the only female among Japan's seven gods of luck, is also the goddess of romantic happiness. In a tale from Kyoto, Benten acted as go-between for a handsome young man and his bride by appealing to the god of marriage, who tied his red cord around them.

the cakes would be placed in green boxes with the characters for "five sons and two daughters," enumerating to the hoped-for outcome of the marriage. Many Chinese bakeries in American cities prepare such cakes by special order. Cookies or pastries might be ordered instead. One Chinese-American couple announced their news to both their families with sweets, sending flaky Chinese pastry to his side, Western sponge cake to hers.

For the recipients of the sweets, etiquette may be tricky. Gifts are expected in return if the sweets are elaborately boxed. The fancier the box, the more expensive the return gift should be. At the very least, cakes, cookies, and pastries signal to close family and friends that the wedding festivities are about to begin.

The Power of Love

Your journey as a married couple has begun. The ancient betrothal rituals recognized and celebrated the transformation of two individuals into one pair, of youths into adults. In the minds of our ancestors, an engagement was meant not to be broken, but to be nurtured as a marriage is nurtured. The elaborate gifts and ceremonies, the contracts and letters, were designed to seal a commitment that, in modern times, has become a difficult pledge indeed.

There is a power to that commitment and to your love. Countless Asian fairy tales glorify the strong bonds of married love, like this Japanese story: A young woman named O-Tei was engaged to a young man, but before they could be married, she fell ill with consumption. On the evening before her death, she promised she would return to the young man with a stronger body. He, in turn, vowed to marry her then.

After her death, he wrote down his promise, sealed the note, and put it on her memorial tablet. Years went by. At the urging of his family, the young man married another woman and had a child. His parents soon died, followed by his wife and child.

Trying to find a way to heal his overwhelming grief, the young man left his town and found his way to a small village. At an inn, he was waited on by a woman who looked very much like O-Tei. Although he had been fond of his wife, his heart had remained loyal to his first love, and so he asked the woman's name.

She said her name was O-Tei, in a voice he remembered well. She knew of the promise he had left at her grave, and that vow had allowed her spirit to return. The woman then fainted. When she awoke, she had no memory of their initial conversation or her former life. The two fell in love and were finally, joyfully married soon after.

May your love be as enduring as that of O-Tei and her husband.

Chapter Three

THE ART OF MARRIAGE

*The journey of a thousand miles must begin with a
single step.*

—LAO-TZU (SIXTH CENTURY B.C.)

*There is always something to upset the most careful
of human calculations.*

—IHARA SAIKAKU (1642–1693)

PLANNING A WEDDING, in any culture, is a long, detailed labor of love. In
Japan, where most weddings are held in special halls, a consultant plans the entire
day, from the solemn Shinto ceremony in the hall's shrine to the last wave good-bye.
Wedding halls, now part of a huge industry in Japan, evolved from humble *gojokai,*
or mutual aid clubs. The first opened in 1948 in Yokosuka as a way to guarantee
low-cost weddings and funerals. Members paid modest monthly installments over a
period of ten years. On the occasion of a wedding or funeral, the *gojokai* supplied

all the necessary items and services for the ceremony. For weddings, it provided the food and the wedding dress.

These days, Japan's wedding halls can orchestrate the wedding of your dreams. While the guest list is up to you, the hall's employees can help with everything from the menu to the music to the gifts for your guests. In the United States, some Asian restaurants offer professional help in planning ethnic ceremonies. The Palisadium, in Fort Lee, New Jersey, for example, has a full-time Korean-American wedding planner who can provide traditional costumes, taped Korean music for the ceremony, and plenty of advice on customs and etiquette.

The majority of couples in the United States plan their own weddings and hope they haven't ordered a too small wedding cake or forgotten to invite anyone. With so many things to remember, a bride can easily become overwhelmed or frustrated by the task. Try to stay calm. The seemingly endless details and sleepless nights will pale in your memory compared with the actual wedding day. The Koreans have a saying, "Don't forget the bridegroom at the wedding home." The traditional Korean wedding included banquets and parties that carried on for days and days. The bridegroom, who was considered the most important person at the wedding, was sometimes lost in the daze of festivities. So that saying means, Don't forget what's important: something to think about during your next sleepless night!

Setting the Wedding Date: Auspicious Days of the Year

One of the first decisions you and your fiancé will have to make is the wedding date. Long ago in Asia, couples had a little help from the gods, who were called upon to advise on the perfect time to be married. It was no small matter: without the gods' approval, the

Tips from an Ethnic Wedding Planner

FROM CATHERINE MATSUMOTO, a professional wedding planner in the Los Angeles area, here are some essential hints for putting it all together:

• *Make a checklist of special items you need.*

ITEM	WHERE YOU GET IT	RESPONSIBLE PERSON
Three-layered sake cup	*Shop in Los Angeles*	*Auntie Kyoko*
Hair ornaments	*Japan*	*Grandma*

• *Prepare a step-by-step run-through of the wedding day.* This is critical for a smooth, well-organized day, says Matsumoto. Knowing what things will look like will leave you less anxious and more in control of unexpected surprises. It will also let you fill in some details you might otherwise forget. Sit down with a sheet of paper and make a schedule. It might look something like this:

8:30 A.M.	Visit hairdresser and makeup person with bridesmaids.
10:30 A.M.	Get dressed. *Spend some time with family.*
Noon	Take formal pictures.
2:00 P.M.	Relax. *Eat something.*
2:30 P.M.	Limo arrives.

3:00 P.M.	Ceremony begins.
5:00 P.M.	Cocktails for guests. *Change into traditional costume.*
5:30 P.M.	Chinese tea ceremony at banquet hall. *Don't forget to review setup with restaurant manager.*
6:30 P.M.	First dance, followed by dinner.
7:00 P.M.	Start making table rounds.
8:00 P.M.	Cut wedding cake. *Change into third dress.*
10:00 P.M.	Leave reception. *Give flowers to moms and dads.*

Go over your timetable with the restaurant manager and the photographer. You might also let your bridesmaids and groomsmen in on the plans. With even a rough schedule in mind, you'll breeze through your perfect day with the confidence of an actress knowing all her cues.

• *Hire a wedding consultant.* If you need additional help, you can engage a professional to plan the day, or just a part of it. There are various fee structures, but most wedding consultants charge between ten and fifteen percent of what they arrange. So, for example, if the consultant finds a photographer, a florist, and a band for $10,000, she'll charge you $1,000 to $1,500. If that seems like a lot, remember that some consultants can help you save money by arranging discounts from vendors or suggesting less expensive ways to create the look you want.

To find an ethnic wedding consultant, ask friends whose weddings you have admired. Or inquire at a local ethnic school or church. For more help, call the Association of Bridal Consultants at 203-355-0464.

Invitations: Creating a Unique Style

Your wedding style begins with your invitation. It is the first impression your guests receive, a lasting memento of your happy day. If you're mixing the traditions of East and West, your invitation may be a lovely place to express the uniqueness of the event. My wedding invitation had a misty painting of cranes in flight over a peaceful, flower-strewn lake. While my husband and I had little idea of the symbolism, the image conveyed our vision for the day. For the lettering, instead of traditional italic type, we chose a more artistic version to match the Oriental feel of the image.

We were fortunate to find our invitation at a local stationery store. If you can't find anything that suits you, custom-design an invitation yourself. One couple I know of used a painting created especially for them on their invitation. Another couple used a photograph of themselves. Remember to match the style of your invitation to your overall wedding scheme.

If you'd like invitations printed with Asian characters, you can find specialty stationery stores and printers that offer this service. One Chinese-American couple issued the traditional invitation, in Chinese characters and English, on red paper with gold

marriage was doomed to failure. For the Chinese, the date was divined at the same time the couple sought approval to marry. In Japan, even today, families go to the *yuino* with lists of auspicious dates to choose from.

Setting a date can be as simple as opening a calendar and choosing the first free Sunday in June. It becomes more complicated when you coordinate dates with your three best friends and your groom's relatives from Seoul, the schedules of your church and your favorite restaurant, and of course, your grandmother's "lucky" time. In Shanghai, couples rush to marry on May 18. Why? The date five-one-eight, or *wu yao ba*, sounds like *wu yao fa*, "I will get rich." Young couples hoping to lock in their chances for wealth fill to capacity the city's wedding halls and restaurants.

Narrow down your dates by choosing first the time of year. For the Chinese, this is after the first new moon in early spring. The Koreans favor autumn, after the harvest season. The Japanese prefer spring or fall—the summers are deemed too hot, and winter is filled with festivals such as New Year's, the most important holiday in Japan.

Once the time of year is settled, the Japanese family turns to the *koyomi*. This ancient astrological calendar, based on lunar months, was used exclusively in Japan before the introduction of the Western calendar in 1872; now it is consulted only for ceremonial events such as weddings and funerals. The year is separated into six-day cycles in the *koyomi,* and each day is labeled as suitable or unsuitable for certain events. Taian and Tomobiki are the most auspicious days for weddings, Butsumetsu is considered unlucky, and the other three days are neutral.

To make matters more difficult, most Japanese now prefer to be married on Sunday. With their six-day work week, this is a day of rest, when the most people will be able to attend. There are, however, relatively few Sundays that coincide with the lucky Taian or Tomobiki, and fewer still in fall and spring. To book a wedding hall, many couples must schedule their weddings for a more neutral day.

Most young couples say they don't put any stock in superstitions. Astrological calendars and fortune-tellers are as outdated as their grandmother's fairy tales and fables. But in the end, weddings are about tradition. Many young people fear upsetting older relatives or *nakodo* who hold these beliefs. My mother pleaded with me to avoid the seventh month, when, the Chinese believe, the dead roam among the living. That sounded unlucky to my Caucasian fiancé and me, so we did as my mother wished. Besides, there's never any harm in sticking with the gods.

A Year to Plan, Month by Month

After setting the date, it's time to get yourself organized. If you want to incorporate ancient customs into your wedding, you must be very careful in your planning. You may have to rent, purchase, or create traditional costumes. Special attention may be needed to prepare antique family clothing. Such items as a Japanese handwoven silk *obi*, or sash, are very delicate; only a few places around the country would iron it. You may have to track down or order wedding artifacts. And finding people to perform special ceremonies takes time.

As you compile the necessary information, choose a system to keep yourself organized. Jot down all your notes in one notebook. Dedicate a calendar to keep track of dates. Or use file folders to follow up on the various services, from reception hall to photographer. One consultant recommends keeping your notes in a three-ring binder, with folders for receipts and contracts. There are also a number of computer programs to keep you organized. You'll be handling a lot of material, from vendor information to sample tapes of bands and disk jockeys, so the more organized you are from the start, the less daunting the task will seem.

Use the following checklists as rough guides to planning your wedding. These are only general recommendations; you should adapt the list to your personal needs.

ink. (Beware: Another couple sent out invitations printed in red ink, only to have a relative inform them that red ink—which looks like blood—was not appropriate.) You can also combine languages, printing foreign characters on one page and English letters on the facing page. For this you'll need to supply the printer with a clear copy of your Oriental script and your English text with the order for the invitations. A Chinese-American couple had their invitations printed on handmade Japanese *washi* paper flecked with gold and silver leaf. The Chinese "double happiness" character graced the front, and on the back, guests were invited to the wedding in English and Chinese.

Many traditional Japanese wedding ceremonies are attended only by close family and friends. If you're having a private ceremony, you may want to send special invitations to the select guests. In that case, the main invitation would be for the reception, with a ceremony card enclosed for the select guests. Or, as is done in Japan, you may send two separate invitations. If you're having a traditional Chinese tea ceremony at a different place or on a different day, you may enclose a ceremony card or send out separate invitations; if the guest is invited to both ceremony and reception, one invitation will suffice.

• Choose an engagement ring with your fiancé, if you haven't already done so. If you're designing your own wedding rings, contact a designer now.

• Visit a fortune-teller, if you desire.

• Announce your engagement to family and friends. Order traditional announcement cakes (Chinese) or traditional announcement gifts (Japanese, Korean). Inform your local or regional ethnic newspaper.

• Celebrate your engagement with a gathering of family and friends.

• Select a wedding date and time. For this, you may want to visit a fortune-teller or use an almanac of auspicious days.

• Set a preliminary budget. Consult with your families about whether you will follow Eastern or Western traditions for paying.

• Sketch out your ideal wedding. Formal or simple? Grand or intimate? Eastern or Western, or a little of both? Shinto or Christian? Reception at home or at a restaurant?

• Reserve your ceremony and reception locations.

• Determine who will officiate at your ceremony or ceremonies.

• Choose your bridal attendants, ushers, and other special people who will participate in the ceremony or ceremonies.

• Hire a wedding consultant, if you wish.

• Plan the reception. Check catering facilities, particularly if you're ordering special food. Give yourself time to gather any unique elements you might want, such as banners or origami cranes.

- Select a caterer, if needed. Request any ethnic dishes you want on the menu, including wedding cakes.

- Choose a photographer and/or videographer. Ask if he or she can take formal portraits of you and your fiancé in your traditional costume before the wedding.

- Select a florist. Inform the florist of any ceremonies that might require flowers, and give him or her a picture or description of your dress.

- Choose your dress(es) and headpiece(s). If you and your groom are alternating between traditional costume and other dress, purchase, rent, or otherwise arrange for all the outfits.

- Select your attendants' dresses.

- Compile names and addresses of guests.

- Begin planning your honeymoon.

FOUR MONTHS IN ADVANCE

- Select and order your invitations. Allow more time if you're printing your invitations in a language other than English or with special paper or ink.

- Finalize the guest list. If you're inviting select people to a tea or Shinto ceremony or other event, make a separate list.

- Order all bridal accessories.

- Select and reserve the outfits for the groom's party.

- Check the marriage requirements for your state. You may need a blood test and physical exam before the state issues you a license.

Adding Asian-looking borders or imprints—or perhaps your family's crest—is one way to personalize your invitation or stationery.

- Choose and purchase wedding rings for each other. (If you're designing your own rings, contact a jeweler in advance.)

- Register for wedding gifts. For ethnic gifts, you may want to register with an Asian department store.

Two Months in Advance

- Address and mail invitations and announcements four to six weeks before the wedding. Invitations to any separate ceremony, such as a tea ceremony, should be sent out at the same time, but not necessarily in the same envelope.

- Complete the details of the ceremony with the person(s) who will officiate. Make sure you have everything needed for any special services.

- Finalize all details with reception hall manager, caterer, musicians, photographer, florist, limousine service, and so on. Order the wedding cake, if it's not to be supplied by the restaurant or caterer; ethnic cakes and other sweets may require more time.

- Arrange the rehearsal and rehearsal dinner. If, as is traditional, the groom's family is hosting the dinner, ask whether they need anything from you. You may want to add some cultural touches to this intimate family gathering. (See chapter 4.)

- Plan the "sisters' party" for your bridesmaids and close friends, if you desire. (See chapter 4.)

- Make appointments with hairdresser and makeup person. Talk to them about special techniques for Asian-Americans and your traditional costume.

- Arrange accommodations for out-of-town guests. Inform the hotels if you have any non-English-speaking guests; they may wish to hire translators for the weekend. If you want to book rooms in a popular area or at a popular time, you may need to reserve them even earlier than now.

- Finalize your honeymoon plans. If you're traveling to a popular destination, you may need to make reservations much earlier than now.

ONE MONTH IN ADVANCE

- Have a final fitting for the wedding dress(es), the groom's suit(s), the attendants' gowns, and the groomsmen's attire.

- Get your marriage license.

- Make transportation arrangements (carpools, willing drivers, and so on) for the wedding day. This may include shuttling out-of-town relatives and guests.

- Ask a friend or relative to serve as translator for any non-English-speaking guests.

- Purchase gifts for each other, the wedding party, and both sets of parents. Keep traditional themes in mind for a more personal gift.

- Hold the "sisters' party" and bachelor's party.

- Visit the photographer for a formal portrait.

- Gather and fill out forms to change your name or address.

- Consult with an attorney on the appropriate changes to make on your will, insurance, bank accounts, and anything else with a beneficiary.

- Send out thank-you notes for gifts received.

The Chinese artist Yang Yan Ping painted this for my husband and me as a wedding gift. We were married in the Year of the Horse, so the Chinese characters for "man" and "woman" ride on the "horse."

The character **shuang-hsi**—*double happiness—a favorite Chinese wedding symbol, is displayed on everything from banners to jewelry.*

Two Weeks in Advance

• Confirm accommodations for out-of-town guests.

• Arrange to have your gifts and belongings moved to your new home.

• Write a wedding announcement for the newspaper, and submit it.

• Address announcements for people who are not invited to the wedding, to be sent on the wedding day.

One Week in Advance

• Have a friend or relative contact the invitees who have not responded. Give a final count of guests to the caterer or reception hall manager.

• Confirm your plans with all vendors—caterer, photographer, florist, musicians, limousine company, and so on. Review any special arrangements or ceremonies with which they may not be familiar.

• Plan the seating arrangements. If you're going to have a special ceremony at the reception, arrange the seating accordingly.

• Make sure the wedding party members have their outfits and accessories.

• Confirm all honeymoon plans. Pack for the honeymoon. Remind the best man to put the honeymoon luggage in the getaway car, or wherever needed, in advance.

• Attend the rehearsal and the rehearsal dinner. Go over any special duties with the wedding party, such as assisting in ethnic ceremonies or special seating arrangements. If you're changing clothes, appoint someone to carry your change of clothes to the reception area. And be sure to spend some time thanking your parents, friends, and family members.

WEDDING DAY

• Set aside time to relax. Take a long bath or try some relaxation exercises.

• Give the best man the bride's ring, the payments for the ceremony officials and limousine driver, and the marriage license. Give the maid of honor the groom's ring.

• Leave yourself plenty of time to get ready. If you're taking formal photographs before the ceremony, allow time between the photo shoot and the ceremony.

• Enjoy yourself!

Chapter Four

OFFERINGS
AND CELEBRATIONS

IN MODERN TAIWAN, the wedding celebration begins with the parade of

gifts from the groom's family to the bride's. Her family hangs a red cloth over the

front door of the house to announce the news to the neighborhood. Family and

friends—especially happily married friends, who might share their fortune with the

couple—are invited over to admire the many offerings.

At an auspicious time chosen by the fortune-teller, a woman (sometimes a

relative, sometimes a friend blessed with wealth and a happy marriage) helps the

bride serve sugared tea to the groom and his family. The tea is special; its sweetness

is a wish for sweet relations between the bride and her new family. In the traditional tea ceremony, the bride serves tea to each family member, oldest to youngest, offering the cup with both hands and a small bow, calling each relative by the proper family name, such as Third Uncle or Second Auntie. After the tea has been sipped, the cup and saucer are offered back to the bride with a lucky red envelope, *hung bao,* stuffed with money.

At the conclusion of the ceremony, the banquet begins. The groom is introduced to the bride's family by toasts. During the meal, the bride's family may distribute boxes of dragon-and-phoenix cakes (the dragon and the phoenix are traditional symbols of the groom and the bride, respectively) to relatives. The groom's family slips away quietly, without a farewell: it is believed that saying good-bye brings bad luck to both families.

Even in the past, when young women had no say in whom they married or how, the period before the wedding was filled with great family banquets and intimate gatherings among close friends. It was an exciting time: the whole household hummed with activity. Wedding clothes of the finest silk and with delicate embroidery were made or purchased. An extensive dowry of money, jewelry, clothing, and household goods was gathered. (In Korea and Japan, the bride's family was expected to provide everything the couple needed to live, from furniture to kitchenware. Today that might include a refrigerator or a television.)

A few days before the wedding, the dowry was moved to the groom's family's home in a festive parade meant to display the riches of the bride. In old China and Taiwan, the bride's family even sent people to the groom's home to decorate the couple's bedroom! Today you may see the dowry parade in the form of a truck with a glass enclosure so onlookers can see the many gifts. (The groom, by the way, isn't exempt from this preparation. He is supposed to secure the house for the couple.)

Nowadays in Asia, the parties begin in earnest two or three days before the wedding. In Japan, the guests may enjoy festive foods, including pastries such as *kohaku manjyu,* red or white buns

This goose, painted by a Japanese artist in the eighteenth century, shows a Western influence. The artist's name is signed in the upper right-hand corner in both Japanese and Dutch.

THE RAT'S WEDDING AND OTHER FABLES

Around the New Year in China, young children are told that if they're very, very quiet, they may be able to hear the sounds of the rat's wedding party. Rats and other rodents are hardly welcome guests, and Chinese hang up pictures of this farcical event as a talisman to chase the rats away.

According to the folktale, on three days of the year—and the nineteenth day of the first month and the third and seventh days of the twelfth month—rats marry. If their weddings go off without interruption, the grateful rats leave the household alone for the year. So special care was taken on these three days to leave the rats to themselves.

Rats appear also in fables from Japan and Korea that illustrate the emphasis on marriage between people of equal social stature. In Japan especially, marriage is a public statement of the status of both households: there, you truly are who you marry. Today the painstaking search for a spouse of similar background is a lingering trace of this custom.

The Japanese rat story goes like this: Mr. and Mrs. Rat were determined to marry their daughter off to the highest-ranking individual they could find. First, they approached the Sun, who shines over all creation. But Mr. Sun declined the title of highest

filled with sweet bean paste, and sake. In China, both sides of the family hold banquets for visiting friends and relatives a few days before the wedding. In the past, the generous groom's family would sometimes send presents of fish, pork, and sweetmeats to provide for the bride's guests. In a ritual held at dusk the day before the wedding, the bride would say a final good-bye to her ancestors, paying her respects at her family's altar.

In Western tradition too, the time before a wedding is an opportunity for family and friends to celebrate. From a small brunch with bridesmaids to an elegant sitdown rehearsal dinner, parties give family and friends a way to show their affection and best wishes. Gifts are often given, for the couple or for their future home. Below are descriptions of traditional wedding gatherings, but feel free to dream up your own. This is an ideal time to introduce family members to one another and to share your heritage with your new family.

I know of one Chinese-American couple who held a "cookie gathering," where the traditional engagement cakes were given out. Instead of having the groom's family drop off the cakes and leave, the bride's family invited everyone in for tea. The party allowed both sides of the extended family to get to know each other better, and to share symbolic foods such as roast pig and lotus and winter melon seeds. When they met later at the wedding, they met as old friends, not new family.

Showers: Traditional and Contemporary

Bridal showers are intimate parties given by friends to "shower" the bride-to-be with gifts. According to legend—Western legend, that is—bridal showers began when a Dutch miller refused to let his son marry a young lady because her father couldn't afford a dowry. Upon hearing of this sad affair, the villagers showered gifts on the couple, thus enabling them to set up house.

Modern showers help couples set up their new life together.

rank, saying Mr. Cloud must be higher, because he could obscure the Sun. Mr. Cloud gave deference to Mr. Wind, who could blow him where he wished. And Mr. Wind deferred to a large stone statue of the Buddha, which the most ferocious gust could not budge from its place.

So Mr. and Mrs. Rat approached the statue, which also declined. In a most gentle voice, the Buddha statue said, "If you're looking for an individual of high rank, look at the rats who live at my feet. In a few years, I will topple to the ground because of their effort and work. Surely, they must be of very high rank."

Mr. and Mrs. Rat returned home that day and married their daughter off to a very eligible rat.

Household items such as linen and kitchenware, and sexy lingerie are traditional shower gifts. For the couple with all the basics, the hostess may set a theme for the gifts, such as gardening supplies or camping gear or gourmet cooking items.

Showers were once women-only affairs. Hosted by a dear friend of the bride or the maid of honor, they were an occasion to enjoy the warmth and bonding among close female friends. Showers once provided an opportunity for married women to pass along wisdom to ease the bride's transition into wedded life. Today, couple showers, where the groom and his friends are invited along with husbands and boyfriends of female guests, are becoming more and more common.

May my dream of you, my love,
Hop on the cricket spirit in flight

Crawl into your bedroom
In the long crisp autumnal night

And rouse you up from the deep
sleep
Bringing me into your sight.

—Park Hyokwan (1781–1880),
Korean poet

Although showers are not an Asian tradition, adding a bit of your culture to the festivities would certainly create a memorable event. From the decorations to the theme to the choice of food, there are a number of ways to highlight the bride's or the groom's Asian heritage. A hostess might consider replacing the Western shower umbrella with an Asian paper umbrella, a Japanese symbol for lovers. A well-decorated tray of traditional offerings, such as Japanese hemp or Chinese candy, would make an interesting centerpiece. The less elaborate ripe millet stalks of Korean tradition can be placed on tabletops or on the gift table. (If you can't find millet, wheat or corn will do.) Flowers with an Asian flair—orchids or lilies—can grace the room or be placed attractively on a Victorian sun hat. Guests might consider offering fun gifts such as goldfish or wooden ducks. Recipes, personal notes, or cash can be given in beautiful Japanese envelopes, *shugi-bukuro.*

If the hostess wants to be very traditional, she might consider asking the bride's or the groom's parents for their own customs, which can vary from region to region. It doesn't take a lot of time or energy to give a nod to a couple's heritage. Let your sense of style and taste be your guide. Often, even the smallest of details can make an event special and memorable.

A Gathering of Sisters: The Bridesmaids' Party

This event can be hosted by the bridesmaids for the bride or by the bride for the bridesmaids. Originally intended as a "farewell to virginity," such parties are now a chance for the bride to celebrate her upcoming wedding with her closest female friends, and to thank her bridesmaids for the work and the support they've given over the engagement period. If you've purchased gifts for your friends—pieces

On her third to the last evening at home, MaMa dressed in white. A lucky old woman, who had a good woman's long life, helped her wash her hair, though this being modern days she only sprinkled water on her head. Dressed in white, MaMa sat behind her bedcurtains to sing-and-weep. "Come and hear the bride cry," the village women invited one another. "Hurry. Hurry. The bride's started singing-and-crying." "Listen. Listen. The bride's singing. The bride's weeping." They sat around the bed to listen as if they were at the opera. The girl children sat too; they would learn the old and new songs. . . .

The women punctuated her long complaints with clangs of pot lids for cymbals. The rhymes made them laugh. MaMa wailed, her eyes wet, and sang as she laughed and cried, mourned, joked, praised, found the appropriate old songs and invented new songs in melismata of singing and keening. She sang for three evenings. The length of her laments that ended in sobs and laughter was wonderful to hear.

—Maxine Hong Kingston, *China Men*

of jade jewelry, say, or mahogany keepsake boxes—now would be an appropriate time to give them.

In China, in earlier times, these "sisters'" gatherings were held among intimate female friends and relatives. Marriage then was an uncertain fate: a bride left her family home forever to live with a man she had never met and her new boss—his mother, the matriarch of the house. To relieve some of the anxiety, the bride-to-be was allowed to weep and curse her fate for three days before the wedding, with *kuge*, weeping songs, and *hunge*, marriage laments. These dirges were memorized or prompted by the "sisters" who gathered to hear her sad songs. Crying, weeping, cursing, and laughing—this overflow of emotion continued until, spent at last, the bride was ready to face her fate.

The Bachelor's Farewell Party

The Western-style "farewell to freedom" enjoys a bawdy and boisterous reputation as the groom celebrates—or mourns—his last night with the boys. Usually hosted by the best man and the ushers, the evening does have at least one genteel tradition. At the dinner, the groom proposes a toast to his bride. After drinking the toast, he breaks the glass, so, say the etiquette books, it will never serve a less noble purpose.

In Korean tradition, the groom has his day with the boys as well. After the wedding, when the couple returns to the bride's family's home, the groom is properly introduced to the young men of the clan. There is much good-natured roughhousing, including hanging the groom upside down by his feet and "beating" him until he is rescued by his new in-laws. The pressure on the groom can be intense: according to one book, "If the groom is not deemed witty or generous enough, he will be forced to drink beyond his capacity or be hit with dried fish and sticks." Scholars speculate that this practice may come from a time when brides were kidnapped and the groom was hunted down and punished by the men of her family. More realistically, the ritual may symbolize the groom's new ties to his wife's family—traditionally, the groom lived for months or years under his in-laws' roof.

The tradition continues in this country as well. A groom is likely to be pummeled by male family members after the *p'ye-baek,* or introduction ceremony—until they are called off by the laughing bride.

Honoring the Family: The Rehearsal Dinner

For a formal wedding, a rehearsal is usually planned for participants the afternoon before the wedding day. Even if there is no rehearsal, it is traditional for the couple, their parents, and attendants to eat together the night before the wedding. Out-of-town guests may be invited, along with close friends and family. Any priest or clergy (and spouse) should also be invited. The dinner is usually hosted by the groom's family.

The more intimate size and informal nature of this dinner makes it ideal for personal touches. Toasts are a must on both sides of the table, with the bride returning any toasts made to her by her fiancé. Guests might take the opportunity to say a few words to the couple or read a poem composed for the occasion, expressing heartfelt wishes that might get lost in the hubbub of the big day. The bridesmaids and ushers might surprise the couple with a photo collage of their dating days, or even a video of old family movies. In Hawaii, Asian-American families often hire professionals to create a slide show of the couple's history to show at wedding events.

Given the presence of both families, the rehearsal dinner is a perfect occasion to pay homage to family customs. The Korean *hahm,* or gift box, is traditionally opened the night before the wed-

According to the experts at Toraya in New York City, a branch of the 450-year-old Japanese bakery that has served emperors, there are two types of *kohaku manjyu,* a special bun served at festive occasions: one made with yams and the other with flour.

The yam version is more difficult to make, as it requires ingredients that are hard to find or duplicate in this country. The flour *manjyu* is simpler: wheat flour is mixed with sugar, Japanese baking powder, and water. (For red *kohaku manjyu,* food coloring is added to the dough.)

A portion of sweet bean paste is then wrapped inside a handful of dough, and a ball shape is formed. Egg white is sprayed or brushed on the dough, and the bun is then steamed for about ten minutes.

ding. If you haven't already exchanged family gifts, this may be a good time to do so. Serving *kohaku manjyu,* round rice buns, or *namagashi,* sweet bean paste formed into flower or symbolic animal shapes, is one way for a Japanese-American couple to round off an evening. Wearing a traditional wedding costume, if you're not saving it for the wedding day, may add color and distinction to an already special event. I wore the traditional red embroidered silk dress, *cheung sam,* to my rehearsal dinner, its brilliant colors winning approval from my old auntie from Malaysia as well as my American-born fiancé.

For the traditional Chinese bride, the night before the wedding is the time to say good-bye to family ancestors. Honor this tradition by paying respect to your parents and family members. You may wish to give them sentimental gifts to show your affection, or thank them in public or private as you make your way from their family altar to begin one of your own.

Special Parties

Lucky for you, there is no end to the kinds of parties that can be thrown for you. A wedding-day breakfast or lunch may allow close friends or relatives to show their love for you, as well as entertain your out-of-town guests when you cannot. Do not feel obliged to attend if you are too busy preparing for the wedding. The hosts and hostesses will understand. Similarly, brunches and lunches held in your honor the day after the wedding may complete the ceremonies.

If you're planning a Western wedding, you still may wish to hold a Chinese tea ceremony, a *p'ye-baek* (the Korean introduction ceremony), or a *san-san-kudo* (the Japanese marriage vow ceremony; see chapter six for detailed descriptions) at a more private party. By dedicating a night or afternoon to honoring your culture, you can include relatives who do not speak English or who are unfamiliar with Western customs. One Korean-American couple had a novel idea: they threw a second, more rambunctious party late into the night after the reception. At the party, their friends coaxed them into playing a few of the more risqué wedding-night games—a custom the Chinese call, for good reason, "warming up the bedchamber."

If you're marrying someone from a different culture, sharing your marriage customs is a good way to introduce each other (or yourselves!) to your heritages. One couple celebrated their different roots with a tea ceremony for her side of the family, the soft cry of bagpipes at the wedding for his. By incorporating such special touches into your wedding celebration, you show your partner that you respect and honor your own culture as well as his, and thus set a pattern for the rich weave of cultures your marriage will create.

Chapter Five

FAMILY, FRIENDS, AND FORTUNE

Without speaking of the Way,
without worrying about the future,
without seeking fame,
here, loving, gazing at each other.

—YOSANO AKIKO,
FROM *TANGLED HAIR*

The Wedding Party

This is your day. Today's best memories will be yours to make, and center stage will belong to you. There are, of course, many people who will play big and small roles at your wedding. Who does what depends largely on which traditions you follow and which people in your life you'd like to honor. Here are the basics.

THE BRIDE

If you're like most brides, visions of floating down the aisle are mixed with nightmares about forgetting to hire a band or sending out invitations late. In Western tradition, the ultimate responsibility for planning a wedding is yours—with help from the grand host and hostess, your parents. In old China, the tradition was the reverse: the groom's mother planned and hosted the gala, which was usually held at her home.

Other details that are your responsibility: choosing your wedding party; organizing a "sisters' party," if you desire; picking out personal gifts for your bridesmaids to thank them for their support; and sending out thank-you notes for the gifts you've received. You may also choose to give a wedding gift to your groom besides his ring. One Chinese-American woman followed the tradition of her mother's village and gave her groom a new wallet, a new belt, and a new suit. Giving gifts to both sets of parents is another nice touch. By Korean tradition, the bride gives substantial gifts to her new in-laws before the wedding. One extravagant woman gave her mother-in-law a mink coat!

Japanese-American brides (and grooms) may wish to follow the tradition of giving gifts, or *hikidemono,* to wedding guests. Wedding favors—the standard gift was a set of dishes—were important offerings, and were often indicative of the family's generosity. Japanese brides spend on average the equivalent of thirty to fifty dollars on each guest's gift.

THE GROOM

While traditionally the groom has fewer responsibilities than the bride, more and more men are having their say in the planning stage. The groom might take charge of choosing the entertainment at the

The sun spirit is male, or yang; the moon spirit is female, or yin. In Taoist thought, the entire universe was created from the marriage of these two forces.

ONE WOMAN'S WORTH

In days of old, Chinese women brought a substantial dowry into a marriage, as Patricia Buckley-Ebrey describes in her book *The Inner Quarters: Marriage and Lives of Chinese Women in the Sung Period.* Cheng Ch'ing-i, married in 1264 at seventeen, came with a hundred acres of land—enough for nearly a dozen tenant families to farm—and a trousseau of luxurious fabrics. (A wealthy Chinese family often gave daughters enough cloth to make their own clothes for life.) Miss Cheng's dowry contained a length of gold-washed, tie-dyed silk, a length of thin green silk for official robes, two bolts of gauze in different patterns, two pairs of top-knot strings, some fifteen pieces of embroidery, and thirty pieces of red tie-dyed cloth. She also brought three sets of ritual books in "double goldfish" bags.

reception or securing a caterer, for example. Or, hand in hand, bride and groom may plan each stage of the day together.

In the West, the groom's first responsibility is to compile the guest list for his side of the family. He also chooses a best man—a brother or close friend, or even his father—and groomsmen or ushers. The groom buys your wedding ring and has it engraved, and obtains the wedding license and arranges the honeymoon. As the wedding day draws closer, the groom should thank his best man and groomsmen with personal gifts, and he should buy a gift for his bride. In some villages in China, the groom would buy new shoes for the younger, unmarried brother of the bride. Together, groom and bride may wish to choose gifts for both sets of parents.

Traditional Asian weddings did not have bridesmaids and groomsmen. There were, however, special people who helped the couple complete the rites. Today, most Asian-American couples ask close friends and family to stand with them as they marry. These attendants are:

MAID/MATRON OF HONOR

This is traditionally the bride's sister or closest friend. As you plan your wedding, your maid of honor (matron, if she's married) may help in any way you wish. She can be a sounding board for ideas or the liaison among your bridesmaids. If you're fortunate, she'll be around to tell you that the dress you just tried on is too frilly, or to whisk you away to a fun lunch when the planning gets overwhelming.

The maid/matron of honor usually arranges and hosts the bridal shower, perhaps with help from relatives and friends. On the wedding day, she may help you dress or make sure you rest before the ceremony. Officially, she is one of two witnesses to sign your wedding certificate. She precedes you down the aisle in a church service and stands next to the groom in any receiving line. You may ask her to help at an ethnic service, pouring tea or lowering you into a deep bow. At the wedding banquet, she is seated at a place of honor to the groom's left, and she has the first dance with the best man.

THE BEST MAN

The best man is often one of the busiest people at the wedding. He holds a position of honor and responsibility, and functions as host, valet, and behind-the-scenes coordinator. He must also coolly and calmly deliver the first toast to the bride and groom.

Before the wedding, the best man is in charge of organizing the bachelor party and, perhaps, buying a joint gift for the couple from the groomsmen. At the rehearsal dinner, the best man may offer the first toast, if the groom's family declines. On the wedding day, the best man has one of the most crucial jobs of all: getting the groom to the church on time, half an hour before the ceremony is to begin. On top of that, he holds the wedding rings, the marriage license, and any tickets for the honeymoon. He also pays the priest, rabbi, or minister, and the limousine driver. (The bride or groom should give him the cash beforehand.)

The best man is one of the two witnesses who sign the marriage certificate. He sits to the bride's right at the banquet and has the first dance with the maid/matron of honor. He is the fourth in line to dance with the bride—after the groom, her father, and her father-in-law. He may help in any ethnic ceremony.

Finally, if you're going on your honeymoon, this cherished and (one hopes) responsible friend packs up and drives your getaway car, hands over the tickets, shakes your hands, and sees you on your way.

BRIDESMAIDS AND USHERS

These attendants have few official duties. Chosen from among treasured friends and close relatives, they are there to witness your vows and help you through your big day. Before the wedding, they may run errands for you, host showers and parties, and offer you a joint gift. In the West, bridesmaids and ushers pay for their own wedding outfits, which usually match those worn by the maid of honor and the best man, respectively. In Japanese tradition, however, the bride and groom foot the bill for all wedding participants. It is deemed impolite to burden guests with any financial responsibilities.

On the wedding day, the bridesmaids attend to the bride while the ushers seat the guests. Offering an arm to the women and escorting the men, the usher seats the bride's guests on the left of the hall, the groom's on the right. Special guests may have cards designating their places. The couple's close family members should be seated toward the front of the hall, immediate family in the front row. To speed things along at a large wedding, you should count on at least one usher per fifty guests. Ushers and bridesmaids may have other duties during an ethnic service. In keeping with Chinese tradition, they may hold an umbrella above the bride's head while she is whisked from her family's home, or say a few words at the Korean *p'ye-baek* ceremony.

At the banquet, these close friends may offer toasts to the happy couple, following the best man.

THE PARENTS OF THE BRIDE

The bride's parents are the hosts of the traditional Western wedding. To honor her high station, the mother of the bride is the last person to be escorted to her seat in a church service and the first escorted out. She stands in the receiving line and, with her husband, hosts the banquet. The bride's father is not required to stand in the receiving

There are many stories about mandarin ducks, those stately birds which mate for life. One is told about a man, who, in search of food, kills a male duck on the banks of a river. That night, he dreams that a beautiful woman comes into his room, weeping and inconsolable. She accuses him of killing her husband and demands he return to the scene of his hunting expedition to see what he has done.

The dream is so real that the man goes back to the riverbank the next day. Looking out at the water, he sees a mandarin duck swimming alone. To his surprise, the duck steps onto the bank at his feet. She drops her head, tears open her breast with her beak, and kills herself. The man feels so remorseful he becomes a celibate priest.

line, but may mingle with the guests. He is the last to wave good-bye to them at the reception.

Before the wedding, your parents may help with the plans, especially if they control the budget. They should be invited to any honorary parties or showers held for you. Your mother is free to

Who Pays for What? Western Traditions

If you decide to follow the Western style of dividing costs, here's the formal breakdown from the Association of Bridal Consultants:

BRIDE

Bridegroom's wedding ring
Bridesmaids' party
Presents for her attendants
Housing for her out-of-town
    attendants
Her hairstylist and makeup person
Her doctor's fees, if necessary
Stationery for personal notes and
    thank-you notes
Wedding gift book and guest book
Wedding gift for the bridegroom
Gift for both sets of parents, if
    desired

BRIDE'S FAMILY

Invitations, announcements, and
    enclosures
Engagement party
Bride's wedding clothes and
    trousseau
Church/temple/synagogue rental
    fee
Reception
Flowers for ceremony and recep-
    tion
Bouquets or corsages for brides-
    maids, honor attendants and
    flower girls
Flowers sent to any hostess enter-
    taining for the bride and bride-
    groom
Corsages given to any friend
    helping at the reception

choose her outfit, and may coordinate colors and styles with the groom's mother and/or your bridesmaids. Your father should be dressed in a style similar to that of the groom and his party.

In old China, the bride's parents sometimes were not even invited to the wedding. (They might host their own celebration, however.) It was they who were losing a daughter, without clearly gaining a son. Some traditions called for the new son to pay respects to his bride's parents before he took her away for the wedding. He came to call on the morning of the wedding day, bringing gifts and finery. He would bow low to his new in-laws, pay his respects to their ancestors, and drink tea, before whisking the bride away to his home. A few days after the wedding, the newlyweds returned to the bride's parents' home to pay their respects.

A bride in Japan's Heian period (794–1185) did not leave her parents' home immediately after her wedding; usually she stayed until after the birth of her first child, or until her parents stopped full-time work. Thus the wedding was held and hosted by her parents. Later, during the samurai period, the bride left her parents' home for that of her husband's parents, and even lighted bonfires at her parents' gate—a funeral tradition—to show that she was never to return. The wedding ceremony, including the libation from the triple-layered sake cup, or *san-san-kudo,* took place at the groom's parents' home.

In old Korea too, weddings of the nobility were held in the courtyard of the bride's family home. The groom might live with his in-laws for years, until the couple, perhaps with children, moved to the groom's family home to assume responsibilities there. Between the fifteenth and sixteenth centuries, however, practices came more in line with Confucian ideals, and the bride moved immediately to the groom's home. But in contrast to the Japanese custom, the wedding ceremony was still held at the bride's home.

THE PARENTS OF THE GROOM

It was the groom's parents, in recent Asian history, who basked in the limelight. It was they who gained a daughter, someone to carry on the ancestral line, someone to bring honor—and sons—to the family. They were the hosts of the wedding, which they most likely held at their home and financed. In the Korean *p'ye-baek,* the wife bows to her new in-laws and serves them food and tea. Her parents do not take part in this introduction ceremony at all.

In Western tradition, the groom's parents have a smaller role than that of the bride's parents. But they are no less honored or respected. Although the groom's parents are not the main hosts, they

Engagement and wedding photographs
Fees for organist, soloists, and/or sexton
Transportation for bridal party from house to ceremony to reception

BRIDE AND/OR HER FAMILY
Boutonniere for the father of the bride
Music for ceremony and reception
Services of a bridal consultant, if needed
Traffic policeman or security

BRIDEGROOM
Bride's engagement and wedding rings
Bride's bouquet
Flowers for both mothers
Corsages for any female honored guests, such as grandmothers or godmothers
Boutonnieres for his attendants and himself
Gloves, and ascots or ties for his attendants
Housing for out-of-town attendants
Fee for minister, rabbi, or other clergy
Marriage license
His doctor's fees, if necessary
Shipping of wedding presents to the couple's home
Honeymoon
Wedding gift for the bride
Wedding gift for both sets of parents, if desired

(continued)

are on hand to greet guests and receive their congratulations. These days, the groom's parents may offer to finance part of the wedding, and may be true cohosts of this most special day.

The mother of the groom may choose to coordinate her dress with the mother of the bride. In a church wedding, she is seated in the first pew of the groom's side, just before the bride's mother is seated, and usually joins the receiving line. The groom's father is dressed in the style of the groom and the rest of his party.

SPECIAL ATTENDANTS

Various other people may be in your wedding party or may participate in special ceremonies. In the Korean wedding, the bride is helped into the traditional low bow by two women called *chan*. These women are chosen carefully: they must have lived a happy life, so that some of their luck may rub off on the bride.

Japanese-American brides may wish to choose a *nakodo,* the ceremonial go-between. Even if he or she has no specific duties, a close relative, an older friend, or a teacher would be honored to be chosen. The *nakodo* may, according to custom, give the first toast and stand with the bride during the ceremony. *Shuhin,* or "principal guests," could be enlisted to give short, personal speeches at the reception. A *shuhin* could be a current or former boss of the bride or groom, a teacher, or other distinguished guest.

The Chinese tea ceremony might offer other honorary duties to a special friend or relative. My mother's closest sister poured each cup of the special tea, while my father's older brother, the most senior uncle present, explained the ceremony and introduced the participants. As was typical for this family storyteller, my uncle shared both personal wisdom and jokes as the tea was poured, making the ceremony intimate and warm. I am sure some of my aunt's and uncle's luck and love rubbed off on us too.

Children can add a wonderful, and sometimes humorous,

touch to weddings. Who can forget the little flower girl who scatters petals before the bride? Or the ring bearer who holds aloft the rings on a dainty pillow? (You may want to use dummy rings, if the child is apt to wander off!) Pages or train bearers usually come in pairs to hold your train as you walk up and later down the aisle. Older children may also participate in a variety of capacities: junior bridesmaids or groomsmen, for example, may give out programs or handfuls of rice or birdseed to the guests.

Who Pays for What? Eastern Traditions

In Confucian traditions, the groom's family pays for most of the wedding. By their thinking, they are acquiring a daughter to help continue the ancestral line—this contrasts with the European notion that the bride's parents "give away" their daughter. The money and goods offered by the groom's family are considered a "bride price" rather than a "dowry" from the bride's family. In Taiwan, the groom's family may pay as much as half a year's salary for the engagement and wedding.

In modern-day Japan, both sets of parents may help pay for the wedding. That's a good thing too; the average cost of a wedding with a hundred guests is at least $33,000—and that's not including the bride's dress or kimono. The bride and groom may offset those costs with funds of their own, but many usually devote their money to their own needs. The groom buys the engagement ring and pays for the honeymoon. He also may help purchase the couple's future home. The bride pays for an engagement gift for the groom, and uses her remaining funds to buy furniture and other items for their home.

As mentioned earlier, *gojokai,* or mutual aid clubs, were set up to help families defray the high cost of weddings during the hardship years in post–World War II Japan. Their evolution into profit-making wedding halls, which cater to members and nonmembers, has somewhat changed their function. Still, members receive a preferred discount.

Korea also has a form of mutual aid organization that helps offset the cost of the wedding, which is usually split between the bride's and groom's families. Called *kye,* meaning "agreement" or "bond," these cooperatives collect dues from members on a regular basis. The *kye* pools the funds, and members tap into the bank for expenses for such events as weddings, birthday parties, and funerals.

For Asian-Americans in this country, especially those marrying people raised in the Western tradition, the question of who pays for what may be tricky. Sit down with your groom, and both sets of parents if necessary, to decide which tradition to follow. You may want to split the costs of the wedding evenly, or each take responsibility for certain areas. Money is a very touchy subject, so approach the topic gently, with consideration for the traditions involved. Although the Western bride-pays-all custom is softening, etiquette books still coach brides not to ask the groom's parents to contribute but to wait until help is offered. A respectful, mature discussion may help couples and their parents resolve the issue.

Asian-American brides and grooms may also choose to follow certain family or village traditions. One Korean-American woman bought the wedding clothes for the groom's entire family, according to custom. A Japanese-American couple purchased the clothes for the bridal party and family. (They contributed some money for clothes to those who were Caucasian.) To be fair, explain all customs to everyone in both families, so that no one feels hurt or left out.

Saving Face

In all discussions, financial or otherwise, be sensitive to the Asian— and Western—measure of "face." Face is your image in the eyes of other people, an important determination of your standing in society. Losing face is the ultimate threat to your position among your peers. A Chinese-American woman's mother reluctantly agreed to pay for an elaborate Chinese banquet, one more expensive than the groom was willing to shoulder for tradition's sake. In order not to lose face among her family and friends, however, she asked the groom to pretend that he paid for the banquet himself.

Face is a concept we all carry with us, no matter what our culture. It is the traces of the ideas and customs we have been raised with, the pride with which we hold them dear, and our conscious and unconscious worries about how we are perceived by others. A wedding, with its formal traditions and social statements, is an event in which face is extremely important. It is an emotional time, a time when we attempt to define who we are and who we want to become, when we break away from our childhood and look into the future as adults. For the sake of harmony, tread gently on each other's face—and hope that your children and their spouses tread gently on yours.

PART II

To Tie a
Silken Knot

Chapter Six

YOUR WEDDING STYLE

On the hilltop a jeweled path shines fair,
On the back of her skirt are stitched phoenixes male and female,
On the two sleeves of her mantle are seen a pair of crows.
Now fold up her gauze clothes and put them in the clothes box.

—ANCIENT CHINESE BALLAD

I T IS THE DRESS of your dreams. Softest silk, swirls of lace, rustles of taffeta, shiny, rich brocade: whatever your fantasy holds, your wedding dress will make you feel like the most beautiful person in the world. Throughout history, brides have worn their best on their wedding day, the glorious finery a tribute to this quintessential romantic ritual of joining two hearts as one. And your dress too will be special. For you, it will hold the most sentimental of spaces, a personal reflection of the majesty, the love, the sweetness you feel for this most incredible day.

The Delicate Asian Touch

To brides all over the world, the white, Western wedding gown is *the* symbol of romance. It is the dress of fairy tales and princesses. The Crown Princess of Japan married in a Western dress styled by Japanese designer Hanae Mori. Her kimono was the work of a French designer. Even in China and Korea, where white symbolizes death, the all-white wedding dress has become de rigueur, replacing the traditional Chinese red dress and brilliant Korean *wonsam*.

But the calls of the ancients are still heard by many. Some Asian-Americans honor tradition by selecting gowns that reflect the styles of cultures past. Asian and American designers, responding to inner voices of their own, have created stunning wedding gowns of richly patterned silk and brocade, mirroring the styles and textures of traditional costumes. The Japanese bridal designer Yumi Katsura has brought the kimono into the modern era, lifting the long hem off the ground and lightening the layers of heavy silks. The effect is simple and elegant: a gown with the soft drape of a classic kimono, yet adapted for the most modern bride. Another of Katsura's sheath dresses uses a dramatic cloth of hand-pinched silk to create a stylized obi sash and a modern *tsunokakushi,* the traditional headpiece.

Color, vivid or subtle, can evoke the image of traditional costumes. *Vogue* editor turned international designer Vera Wang envisions a bodice of gold lace atop a full skirt of delicate tulle. Anneliese Sharp adds a jacket of lucky red to a strapless white satin gown. For her own upcoming wedding, the Korean-American designer Gemma Kahng is considering a gown of "off-off-off-white, even beige."

The traditional look can be modernized by changing the bright colors to pearly white. Canton-born designer Vivienne Tam imagines a white dress with a dragon and a phoenix, symbols of groom and bride, embroidered in white on the bodice. The white on white, she says, gives the bodice texture and sophistication. On

the bride's head, she would place the traditional headdress of king-fisher feathers and pearls, but again in white. Jade or platinum ear-rings and "many, many bracelets" would be her adornment. "When you mix two cultures," Tam says, "you should create something very interesting, very inspiring, something very courageous."

A gown's cut and silhouette can betray the designer's sen-sibilities. The simplicity of Vera Wang's dresses, with their high, elegant necklines, echoes the dignity of traditional Asian costumes. Korean-American designer C. J. Yoon Ono creates a column dress of pure pearl gray. A long coat with wide sleeves is draped over the dress, recalling the shape of the Korean *wonsam*. The looser fit of Japanese kimonos can be seen in Hanae Mori's gowns. Her evening dresses and bridal wear are not as revealing as those of many of her

As the Chinese immigrated to other countries, they brought their customs and traditions with them. This Malaysian-Chinese bride (circa 1924) wears a traditional kwa from southern China.

The clear, clean lines of the fitted bodice blossom in a full skirt, in this wedding dress by Vera Wang.

C. J. Yoon Ono sculpts a spare sheath dress and drapes it with a spacious coat.

Western counterparts, instead following the straighter body line of the traditional kimono.

Whatever the creation, silk is the material of choice for many of the best bridal designers. Discovered around 2640 B.C. by Lei Tsu, consort of the Yellow Emperor, this queenly fiber favored by the likes of Cleopatra still reigns supreme today. Shimmery shantung, diaphanous organza, delicate damask, luxurious brocade—silk

This late-nineteenth-century bride's headdress, decorated with kingfisher feathers, pearls, and silk tassels, swirls with dragon and phoenix figures. The central element would have been worn dangling over the forehead.

ALAN MIYATAKE ON WEDDING PHOTOGRAPHY

Many Asian-American brides and grooms, says Alan Miyatake (grandson of Toyo Miyatake, known for his searching photos of World War II internment camps), prefer more formal photography. Posed group shots, emphasizing family, are a must for most Asian-American couples; some opt for candids as well.

Formal studio poses are taken a few weeks before the wedding. Asian-American couples who don't want to change into traditional costume during the wedding might have their portraits taken in costume beforehand for faraway relaatives. Some photography studios have traditional garb on hand to rent for the picture.

When comparing prices, look for extra costs, says Miyatake. Some photographers charge more for off-site photos, such as those taken at a tea ceremony, and some charge more for longer receptions.

PHOTO TIPS

• Make sure your photographer and/or videographer have a sched-

can come in a variety of weights, textures, and styles. Traditional wedding costumes were created from this prized fabric, the material of nobility and purity.

You can satisfy the sentimental yearnings for tradition in even simpler ways. Wear Western white, but add distinctive accents to make your dress your own. Spashes of color—bright reds, dazzling gold—can be added with a red rose bouquet, a lucky gold ribbon. Hanae Mori suggests carrying a delicate white fan instead of a bridal bouquet for a clean, modern look. You might carry a ceremonial Japanese dagger or add a long veil to your headpiece, to create a modernized *wataboushi,* the traditional Japanese white face covering. In your hair, wear a tortoiseshell comb decorated with diamonds and pearls. Or, as Vera Wang suggests, wear your hair in an Asian style.

Dress your bridesmaids in Chinese brocaded sheaths in primary colors or in the bright red, indigo, or yellow of traditional Korean dress. Grooms and ushers can follow suit with colorful cummerbunds or ties.

Asian style is simple, says Yoon Ono, with clean, uncluttered lines. A simple bouquet, a simple veil, a simple dress—then all that shines through is you.

Traditional Wedding Costumes for the Bride and Groom

Another way to add tradition to your wedding style if you have chosen Western dress is to change into your ethnic costume during the ceremony or reception. The cool white of the Japanese, the vibrant reds of the Chinese, the jeweled tones of the Koreans: the wedding costumes of Asia are as rich in history and symbolism as they are in color and beauty. As you wrap yourself in the textures, colors, and styles of your ancestors, you honor traditions that have been alive for centuries. Even if you choose not to wear the whole costume, you may wish to borrow from your ancient heritage the symbols of luck, happiness, and marital harmony.

Displaying your ethnic colors is one way to make your wedding day unique. But it can be much more than that. For a Japanese woman, changing from the all-white wedding kimono to a brightly colored and patterned kimono, a process called *ironaoshi,* is a symbolic rebirth. The girl becomes a mature woman, with a new set of

ule of the day's events. Discuss any special ceremonies that the photographer may be unfamiliar with. He or she can then plan the best place and time to get good shots.

• Consider taking your formal shots before the wedding. Although it may spoil the romantic moment when your groom gets his "first" look at you, your guests won't have to wait for you to join them at the reception. Also, says Miyatake, the bridal party looks its best before the ceremony.

• Keep photography in mind when choosing your reception site. Find a beautiful screen for your formal pictures. Or have them taken at a botanical garden or park in your area.

• Slide shows or video movies of the couple, shown at the wedding or rehearsal dinner, have become standard at Asian-American weddings in Hawaii. The presentation might include childhood photos or film footage, interviews with friends and family, and narration and music. A videographer might be able to help you, or you can hire a professional slide-show producer.

• If you choose a formal photo style, make sure your photographer has a list of photos he or she plans to take. Give your photographer a list of important photos you want taken, before the wedding. It's hard to keep track of what photos were taken on the wedding day.

For petite women, the silhouette is the most important consideration, say Yumi Katsura's designers. They recommend high-waisted, A-line gowns, where the skirt flows from under the arms to the floor. The smooth waistline gives smaller women a cleaner silhouette and a taller appearance; too many gathers of fabric (shirring) at the waist make shorter women look stumpy.

If you have your heart set on a full, drop-waisted dress, be sure the waist is not too low. A dress with a too long torso makes a short woman look even shorter. Choose a dress with a drop waist just a few inches below your normal waistline.

If you want more height, rely on your accessories to add inches. Full veils can be gathered on top to give you the illusion of height, for example. Stay away from overwhelming dresses that drown you in yards and yards of fabric. For smaller women, simple is most flattering.

relationships. These days, the groom often changes as well, perhaps to show that in these modern times both the man and the woman separate from their parents' homes and start a new, independent life together.

For Asian-Americans, raised in this country, donning ancient costumes can be a life-affirming gesture, a way to touch hands with their ancestors, their spiritual birthplace. As one Chinese-American, Christine Gorman—who danced the Jewish *hora,* or wedding dance, in a red *cheung sam*—said, "Somehow, it felt right. I felt like myself."

KOREAN

The two bride's dresses were once the costume of the nobility. The simple lime-green *wonsam* and the more elaborate *hwarrot,* or "flower robe," are embroidered with flowers and butterflies, symbolizing happiness, wealth, and nobility. The long, draping sleeves are banded with colors: red, symbolizing heaven; indigo, symbolizing earth; and yellow, symbolizing man. A band of white covers the bride's hands, indicating respect. A lengthy red sash embroidered with a Chinese phoenix, the traditional symbol of marriage, is tied in the back and draped. Underneath, the bride wears a *hanbok,* the doll-like traditional dress of Korea.

The headpiece is a black cap, studded with multicolored gems, including the much-prized jade. The bride wears white socks and embroidered shoes.

On her face are three red circles, or *yonji konji,* about the size of nickels, one on her forehead and one on each cheek. The circles can be drawn with makeup or pasted on. If pasted on, they may be cut from paper or, as is traditional, from dried red peppers. One Korean-American dress shop owner suggests cutting them from rose petals. The circles are supposed to ward off evil spirits.

The groom's *faruotsu* is also the dress of the nobility. It is

Crown Prince Naruhito married career diplomat and Harvard graduate Masako Owada in June 1993. The Crown Prince wore a deep-orange silk court robe, or ouninoho. The Crown Princess wore the traditional multicolored silk kimono of the imperial household, or junihitoe.

made of dark green damask with auspicious symbols woven in gold. The sleeves, like those of the *wonsam* and *hwarrot,* are banded with red and yellow, ending in white. A sash of red damask is tied around the waist. The headdress is the tall black cap of high-ranking officials, made of silk. The traditional shoes are boots, reaching the lower calf.

Traditional wear can be rented from Korean dress shops and even some banquet halls around the United States for about $150 a day. The price includes both the bride's and the groom's outfits, plus any accessories—shoes, headpieces, sashes. A bride might have to supply her own *hanbok.* Grooms can wear a suit under their costume.

Ask a relative in Korea to send you a family heirloom, or buy a new costume and start a tradition of your own.

JAPANESE

The Japanese wedding costume dates back to the Edo era (1700–1900), when brides of samurai would wear the *shiromuku,* the all-white silk kimono. For the Japanese, white symbolizes a new beginning. It also

MICHI TAHARA ON WEDDING MAKEUP

Japanese brides traditionally wore the pasty white makeup and tiny red lips of Kabuki players. (Two famous players, Ichikawa Komazo and Nakayama Tomisabu, are pictured at right.) With no definition on their faces except on the lips, brides presented blank, mysterious images as they drank the wedding sake.

The look of today's bride, no matter where she is from, is natural, fresh, springlike, says New York makeup artist Michi Tahara. Instead of masking a bride's emotions, the makeup should let her inner happiness shine through. Tahara recommends starting with a powder foundation that gives a soft, not shiny, look. Following her Asian tastes, Tahara always wears one shade lighter than her own skin, making sure to carry the foundation down her neck. "Asians prefer lighter skin," she says. To give the flatter Asian face some contour, Tahara uses a foundation one shade darker below the cheekbone.

Now the eyes: Tahara uses a pencil of dark brown or black to define the eye, drawing light lines very close to the upper and lower lashes. She prefers pencils over liquid liners because liquid makes too dark a line. For eye shadow, she uses light, natural colors—browns—to add depth. She darkens the area between the nose and

symbolizes death. In the case of marriage, the bride "dies" as her father's daughter and is reborn a member of a different house and family. Marriage is thus an initiation rite into adulthood.

The wedding kimono has many layers and undergarments. The number of layers in your kimono depends on your class. A commoner wears three layers; Crown Princess Masako, a commoner by birth, wore twelve.

The traditional bride carries a dagger in her sash, or obi; this was added to the wedding kimono during the samurai period. Today the dagger is ceremonial, but its legacy is lethal. If, for some reason, the bride was returned to her family in disgrace, she would use the dagger to commit suicide. Her hair is arranged off her neck and worn with an elaborately styled wig and held up by tortoiseshell combs, symbolizing the long life and many offspring of the steady turtle. (The hairpiece and combs can cost as much as $10,000.) On the way to the shrine, she wears the *tsunokakushi,* a white cloth covering her head's "jealous horns," and the *wataboushi,* a white cloth covering her face. Like the Western veil, these coverings are removed during the ceremony. Her face is painted creamy white, with her lips the only splash of color. The upper lip is small, while the lower lip is full—"so, from the side, she looks like she's smiling," says beauty specialist Jane Aiko Yamano.

At the start of the reception, the bride changes into the *iro-uchikake.* This richly ornate robe, of beautiful golds and silvers, deep reds, and pure white, is embroidered with auspicious symbols such as cranes and flowers. The bride's tortoiseshell hairpieces are replaced with gold and silver ornaments. Toward the end of the reception, the bride changes once again, this time to a deep-colored, highly patterned kimono called a *furisode,* literally "swinging sleeves." This is the last time she is allowed to wear this kind of kimono, reserved for young, unmarried women. The number of times the bride changes depends on the status of the family.

The groom wears a black silk kimono with his family crest, or *mon,* in white in five different places. Under his kimono is a

the eye, and takes the shadow up under the eyebrow bone and out to a point beyond the eye. This brings out the nose and sinks the eyes deeper. A light penciling of the brows finishes off the effect.

For the lips, Tahara recommends shades between pink and red. Red, she says, is a bit strong for weddings.

Miho Kosuda on Choosing Your Flowers

Though Asian weddings traditionally did not use them as ornaments, flowers have become essential to any wedding. They add romance, elegance, and delicate beauty to any event. In some cultures, they are the very symbol of love.

When choosing flowers to accent your dress, says Miho Kosuda, a noted Japanese-American flower stylist for such designers as Bill Blass, take into consideration the dress's color, fabric, and style and your height. If you're planning to wear white, remember that there are many shades of white. The flower should accent the color of your dress and blend in harmoniously with the fabric. A cool white orchid against a creamy ivory dress may make your off-white dress look dirty, Kosuda says; the texture of the elegant calla lily, stunning in its simplicity, highlights the smooth lines of a wool crepe sheath.

Kosuda tries to mimic the dress's style in her designs. The Asian look is simple, even austere, in its beauty. A bride in an Asian-style dress may carry a bouquet of orchids, their elegant petals accentuating the lines of her dress. A gloriously rich purple kimono, the kind worn by a bride at the reception, may show off a simple bouquet of irises. Purple is the color of love in Japan.

striped, pleated skirt, or *hakama*. On top is a *haori* coat with the same five family crests. He carries a white folded fan and wears white sandals.

Many Japanese-Americans still treasure kimonos handed down through the generations. One store dressed a bride in a five-hundred-year-old kimono, a precious family legacy. Quite a few antique kimonos exist in this country, sent over by worried relatives of Japanese-Americans during the harrowing days of World War II.

If you don't have a family kimono, you can rent one from a few stores in the United States. Renting is pricey, though: one store in New York City charges a $1,600 fee, which includes the services of a professional who will dress you (tying a kimono is very tricky; the wraps are tightened by feel) and do your makeup and hair.

CHINESE

On the day before the wedding, the bride's traditional hairstyle is changed from that of an unmarried woman to that of a married woman. A woman who has been blessed with sons removes the fine hairs from the bride's forehead by rolling a piece of red thread over them. The procedure is called *hoi min*, or "opening the face."

On the wedding day, the bride bathes in special herbs such as bamboo, pine, and artemisia (a pungent leaf) to purify her; the herbs symbolize wishes for fortitude, longevity, and prosperity in married life. She is dressed first in white undergarments, meant to be kept for her funeral garments. The style of the wedding dress differs from region to region. In northern China, brides generally wear one-piece dresses. These look like long-sleeved *cheung sam*—the traditional form-hugging, one-piece dresses—but are looser and very elaborately designed. In the south, brides wear the two-piece *hung kwa*, a long decorative jacket over a long embroidered skirt. (In the old days, the ever-practical Chinese would save the skirt to make baby clothes for the first child.)

Kosuda advises you to be aware of your height when choosing a bouquet. The romance of the cascading bouquet, favored by many, can overpower a petite bride. To add a touch of their heritage, Asian-American brides might create a floral design around a folding fan of gold paper or silk. Japanese-American brides might do the same with the traditional dagger.

If you're looking for flowers that can give an Asian flavor, consider phalaenopsis, a white orchid. Though expensive, it's the classic Asian flower. Kosuda often combines it with variegated ivy, to stress the clear lines associated with Asian flower design. Kosuda also favors the white Amazon or Eucharis lily. Chinese-American brides might add a splash of luck to a white Western gown with a round bunch of luscious red roses.

For a headpiece Kosuda suggests tiny white stephanotis or miniature roses. Both flowers are hardy enough to stand up to the heat of the head and the heat of the moment.

If you're carrying orchids, your groom and his groomsmen (and fathers, too) may wear boutonnieres of a single orchid. Whatever flower is used, the groom's boutonniere is usually distinct. Bridesmaids carry bouquets similar to yours. Mothers and grandmothers usually have corsages pinned to their dresses or worn at the wrist.

Chinese wedding dresses are red, a color considered lucky since the Ming dynasty, and are very ornate. Golden phoenixes, the female half of the traditional symbol for bride and groom or empress and emperor, adorn the silk cloth, along with chrysanthemums and peonies, symbols of wealth and good fortune. The *hung kwa* dates back to the Yuan dynasty and was originally intended to be worn only by the imperial family. But, as the story goes, a courtier packing up her old clothes to send to her poor sister was spotted by Kublai Khan. He took pity on the girl and ordered that she be given a *kwa* owned by the imperial family for her sister. Since then, brides have been allowed to wear the *kwa*.

On her head, the bride wears an ornate headdress of gilded silver inlaid with kingfisher feathers and pearls, a "phoenix crown." Before and during the wedding ceremony, her face is covered with red silk cloth, sometimes many layers, to shield her from the heavens. By Chinese tradition, a married women leaves her family's home forever, and is erased from their ancestral tablet. The red veil protects her at this vulnerable time, as she leaves the protection of her family's home and enters that of her husband's family. In her hand the bride carries a folding fan, which she drops on the road outside her parents' house, indicating that she will never return.

The bride may change many times during the ceremony, and this tradition is kept by Chinese-Americans. The many outfits may indicate the wealth of the bride's family. At a lull in the banquet, or before a special ceremony, she changes to another formal dress, usually Western-style. She also wears all the jewelry she owns—a public display of her dowry. In the United States, these obvious riches can pose a threat: some Chinese-American families in California now hire private security guards for weddings!

The groom's costume, as all grooms' costumes, is less elaborate than the bride's. A black silk coat is worn over an embroidered-dragon robe of dark blue. In the past, if the man held a high rank, his badges would decorate the black coat. Commoners wore the blue *cheung sam* under their black coats. A long red sash was draped over one shoulder and tied at the waist; this later would be used as a baby carrier. On his head, the groom wears a black hat with red tassels.

The number of garments worn by the bride and groom was important in ancient China. The bride wore four or six garments, the groom three or five. These numbers matched the all-important yin and yang principles: even numbers for the female yin, odd for the male yang.

Traditional garb can be rented from dress stores around the country for about $600 a night; that covers both the bride's and the groom's costumes. Many couples choose less elaborate traditional wear for the reception, donning the full elaborate costume—the headpieces alone can be quite heavy—only for a formal portrait.

Layers of richly dyed robes in vibrant colors and designs were worn as a sign of a woman's beauty in ancient Japan (Three Contemporary Beauties, *Kitagawa Utamaro*, Edo period, c. 1793).

A Chinese bride's dowry might contain bolts of silk for her clothes—often enough to last a lifetime (Court Ladies Preparing Newly Woven Silk, *attributed to Emperor Huizong, Northern Sung dynasty, early twelfth century*).

Auspicious symbols such as cranes, butterflies, a phoenix, and peonies adorn these panels of Korean wedding robes, made of embroidered silk. The flowering peach tree represents a woman ready to marry (Choson dynasty, 1850–1900).

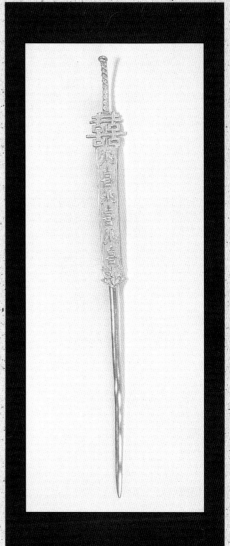

The traditional "double happiness" character is prominent on these gold wedding ornaments from China's Ch'ing dynasty (clockwise from bottom left): fingernail guards, rings, earpick-hairpin, earrings. Butterflies, a symbol of long life and love, also figure in the decoration.

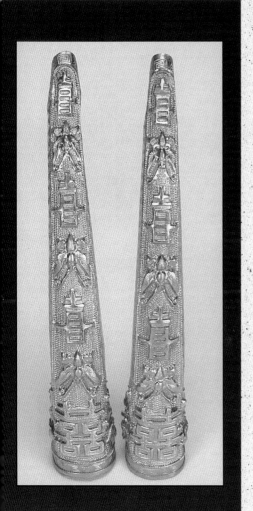

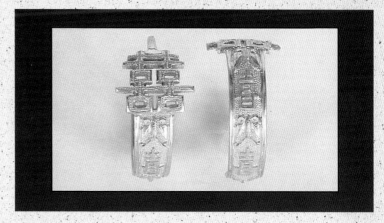

During the wedding reception, the Japanese bride wore a brightly colored furisode. This embroidered satin and silk furisode is from the early nineteenth century.

Ornamental hairpieces have been popular in Japan since the Edo era. They were made mostly from tortoiseshell, which symbolizes long life and many children.

In Asia, grooms too were well adorned. A bridegroom in late-nineteenth-century China would have worn this wedding hat.

Korean brides wear three red dots on their faces, to ward off evil spirits.

For a 1995 group wedding at Taipei's Confucius Temple, Taiwanese couples donned the traditional wedding costume.

The luxurious Korean hwarrot, or "flower robe," was initially worn by brides of the royal family, but soon spread to members of all classes. Embroidered designs of water, rocks, birds, and peonies symbolize wealth, honor, and life.

Japanese brides change dresses several times during the course of the wedding. This bride is wearing a red-and-gold *iro-uchikake,* usually the first change after the white wedding gown. The groom wears the traditional black-and-white *hakama.*

A Korean-American couple in traditional dress: the bride wears a *hwarrot,* the groom a *faruotsu.*

The lucky red of this Chinese bride's bouquet (also in her attendant's dress) adds a traditional accent to her Western gown (bridal gown by Lazaro, bridesmaid's dress by Judd Waddell for Jim Hjelm).

Flower designers can fashion a bouquet with the sharp, spiky look of Asian arrangements. Miho Kosuda's bouquet creates the illusion of a single flower by fusing the petals of many lilies.

Asian-American brides can mix East and West in gowns with traditional styling and accessories, such as these by Yumi Katsura (left) and Ulla-Maija Atelier (below).

Chapter Seven

Two in Body, One in Spirit: The Wedding Ceremony

Before I came to know you, love,
Little my life was worth to me.
I prize it now all things above,
And wish long in this world to be.

—FUJIWARA-NO YOSHITAKA,
FROM *ONE HUNDRED POEMS*
FROM ONE HUNDRED POETS
(THIRTEENTH-CENTURY JAPAN)

IN OLD ASIA, wedding ceremonies were conducted in silence. The bride and groom conveyed with solemn gestures and acts what they did not say in words. In the East, subtlety is prized. The shape of a flower, the depth of a bow, the rhythm of a poem have deeper meanings than the shallow sounds of the tongue. Thus, for the Koreans and the Japanese, a simple sip of sake replaces the words "I do." For the Chinese, the reverent bows to ancestors, family, and each other speak volumes

MUSIC AT YOUR CEREMONY

The classic *Book of Rites* forbids music at weddings, as it disrupts the balance of yin and yang: music leads to movement, which leads to yang, and therefore is not appropriate for brides, who should be yin. Few people followed this rule, however, using music to add to the festivity of the occasion and mark the beginning and end of the various rituals. When Emperor Che-tsung, ruler of China from 1086 to 1100, was married, the empress dowager was told to obey the rulebook. She dismissed this idea, saying, "Even ordinary people, when they take a bride, engage a few musicians." In fact, there was enough music and song at weddings to commonly refer to them as "singing the song of a new groom."

Singing girls dressed in bright, colorful costumes also joined the wedding procession, entertaining the men and playing silly games. One high official in the twelfth century hired forty of them for his son's wedding. For their costumes, he had silk specially dyed in red and purple patterns, each girl's different from the next.

Singing girls might not be appropriate for an American event, but you may want to add Asian-style music or dance to your wedding. Traditional instruments, such as a *pipa,* a Chinese pear-shaped

of the respect, honor, and courtesy of a true joining of souls.

Weddings are much more than just a coming together of individuals. Traditionally in Asia, wedding ceremonies were an initiation into adulthood, symbolizing all the responsibilities that go along with that status. For women especially, marriage marked a change in life. They left the warm embrace of their family, to whom they would not return, and became subject to the demands of a foreign household. A wedding was also a joining of two families and their fortunes. The colorful, and very public, wedding rituals and gift exchanges gave families a chance to display their wealth and social standing.

Most important, a wedding signaled the creation of a new family, where children would be nurtured to continue the family's good name, the ancestral lineage, and the society at large. In Japanese mythology, the male and female deities Izanagi and Izanami married and gave birth to all of creation—a Far Eastern Adam and Eve. According to legend, these two gods, who were brother and sister, came down from the heavens to primeval earth by means of a rainbow bridge. Izanagi plunged his spear into the ocean, and as he took it out, the drops of water that fell off congealed into the island of Ono-koro.

The two gods married on Ono-koro and learned how to make love by watching a pair of wagtails. (The birds have been forever blessed for their lesson: it is said even the god of scarecrows cannot frighten the wagtails.) Out of the union of Izanagi and Izanami came the rest of the Japanese islands, the sun, the moon, mountains, trees, and the wind. The power of the myth is still strong: even today in Japanese agricultural communities, a wedding is a sign of a good harvest.

Your wedding ceremony may not affect the local crop, but it is significant nonetheless. Whether your ceremony is sacred or secular, whether you say "I do" or take a sip of wine, this is the high point of the day. The moment when you are joined as husband and wife is brief, but its impact on you, on your families, and on society will last a lifetime, maybe more.

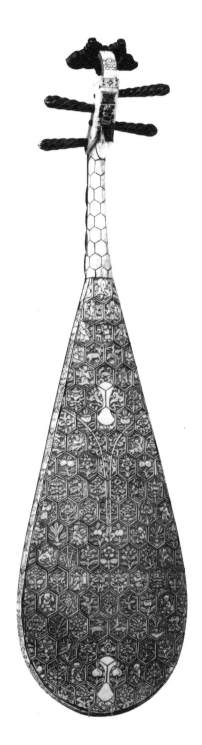

lute, or a *koto*, a Japanese harp, can be played by a professional at the ceremony. The music could be offered softly as background or between readings, like a string quartet. At the reception, you might have a Japanese *od-dio* dancer present her graceful movements, or have a Korean harp, *kayakum*, performance just before your *p'ye-baek* ceremony, to create a new mood. An ensemble of Chinese bamboo flute, or *dizi*, violin, or *erhu*, and *pipa* could be offered during the tea ceremony.

This Chinese lute, or pipa, dates from the Ming dynasty. The word itself describes the back-and-forth motion of the player's right hand across the strings.

The peach tree is young and
elegant;
Brilliant are its flowers.
This young lady is going to her
future home,
And will order well her chamber
and her house.

The peach tree is young and
elegant;
Abundant will be its fruit.
This young lady is going to her
future home,
And will order well her house
and chamber

The peach tree is young and
elegant;
Luxuriant are its leaves.
This young lady is going to her
future home,
And will order well her family.

—Ancient Chinese ode

For me, performing the traditional rites on my wedding day symbolized the new life my husband and I were creating. We had three ceremonies that day: a Christian wedding, a Bahá'í wedding, and the Chinese tea ceremony, or *cha tao*. It was important to us to hold all three. For one, it showed our respect and love for both our families and their traditions. Just as significant, it represented our new family, part Eastern and part Western. Our lives will be different from our parents' lives, different from how we each were raised. By incorporating all our traditions in front of our families and friends and the gods, we were setting our course for our life together, making two different halves into a new whole.

You too may choose to add traditional rites to your wedding ceremony. Some couples hold two different ceremonies, some mix and match. One couple, for example, read a poem in Chinese and translated part of the English-language religious service for their Chinese-speaking guests. A Japanese-American couple held two separate ceremonies, and followed up with a banquet of Japanese and American foods. A Chinese-American couple in Hawaii went traditional from beginning to end, starting the day with the fortune-teller's approval and closing it sipping wine in front of white paper tablets representing heaven and earth.

Gestures of respect, prized in Asian culture, can be sprinkled throughout your day. One Korean-American groom bowed deeply to his father-in-law after the older man walked his daughter down the aisle. Another couple bowed and presented bouquets to their parents after they were pronounced husband and wife in a Western ceremony. A Korean-American couple married in a church service held the traditional *p'ye-baek* at the reception.

In the next few pages, you'll find descriptions of traditional wedding ceremonies. The descriptions are generalized; rituals can vary greatly. Be sure to ask your parents and grandparents about the traditions practiced in their village. As you reach for the stars and the moon, it's good to know where your feet are.

Throughout Yi dynasty times (1392–1910), a peony screen was an essential backdrop for weddings. Even poor peasant families would rent or borrow a screen for the ceremony. Afterward the screen would be placed in the wedding chamber for the first night. The peony, the queen of flowers, is a symbol of happiness, purity, beauty, love, and sex. It also evokes the woman and her sexuality, while the tall, craggy rock upon which the peony is perched suggests the male organ.

The *Kunbere*: The Korean Wedding Ceremony

A Korean bride (foreground, center) kneels at the teresan *as her husband stands on the other side.*

For the Korean couple, the wedding ceremony starts when the groom, resplendent in his wedding finery, meets the bride at her parents' home; the main courtyard of their home was the traditional site for weddings before the eighteenth century. This is the last of the six ceremonies set down by Confucius in his *Book of Rites.* In Korea, it is called *shingei.*

The groom, in a carriage, is accompanied by a happily married man on horseback carrying a live goose, the symbol for marital fidelity. When they arrive at the bride's home, the goose is given to her mother as a sign of the groom's faithfulness.

The couple is escorted to a table, the *teresan,* in an area set off by a screen with images of peonies. On the table are traditional items such as a hen, a rooster, and a bamboo stick, representing fidelity and virtue. The groom stands facing east, the bride facing west. They bow deeply to each other, the bride four times, the groom twice.

The bride's bow is so low that she needs attendants, called *chan,* to help her up and down. With her hands flat in front of her body, one over the other and both covered by the white cloth of her robe, she sinks to her knees and bows her head and body forward, hands and long sleeves held high, covering her face.

After the bows are over, the *chan* pour a special white wine called *jung jong* into cups made from the two halves of a gourd. (In traditional villages, the gourd was grown by the bride's mother.) After the bride and groom take a sip from their separate cups, the wine is mixed together, poured once more into the gourd cups, and tasted again. This is *kunbere,* in effect the wedding vow. By drinking the mixed wine, they are forever joined as one.

Before the eighteenth century and the push toward a more

Confucian ideal, the bride and groom would live at her parents' home. After months, even years, they would move to the groom's family home—perhaps to take over the role of heads of the household.

A few days after the wedding, however, the couple would visit the groom's family to pay respects with the *p'ye-baek* ceremony. In this ceremony, the new wife bows low and presents dates and chestnuts—symbols of children—to her father-in-law and dried meat to her mother-in-law. Father- and mother-in-law sit on the floor beside a low table. On the table are symbolic items: a whole chicken, dried squid cut to resemble beautiful bouquets, and dates, chestnuts, and jujubes.

The parents, in turn, offer sake to their new daughter-in-law, a gift called *ikkon-no-rei*. This is a subtle but significant gift: it is a rare privilege for a younger person to be served by an elder. As a

WEDDING TEA

In China, each village has its own recipe for the sweet wedding tea served at tea ceremonies. One village combines three ingredients boiled together in water, two of which provide a play on words: dried lily bulbs, or *bok hop,* which translates into "a hundred years together"; and dried lotus seeds, or *lian zi,* which sounds like "continuation of sons"; there are also dried red dates, or *hung zao,* whose color brings luck. When the tea is served, two of the three ingredients are placed in a special teacup. For my wedding, we used a red and gold tea set decorated with phoenix and dragon images.

According to an account in *Wild Swans* by Jung Chang, the bride-groom kowtowed five times to the tablets of heaven and earth before heading to the bedchamber alone. Then the bride, Jung Chang's grandmother, curtseyed five times before the tablets, and followed her new husband to the bedroom, where he removed her red veil. As was customary, she stayed in the room until the wedding was over:

The two bridesmaids presented each one of them [the couple] with an empty gourd-shaped vase, which they exchanged with each other, and then the bridesmaids left. Dr. Xia [the groom] and my grandmother sat silently alone together for a while, and then Dr. Xia went out to greet the relatives and guests. My grandmother had to sit, motionless and alone, on the kang *[bed], facing the window, on which was a huge red "double happiness" paper [cutout], for several hours. This was called "sitting happiness in," symbolizing the absence of restlessness that was deemed to be an essential quality for a woman. After all the guests had gone, a young male relative of Dr. Xia's came in and tugged [my grandmother] by the sleeve three times. Only then was she allowed to get down from the* kang.

final gesture, the groom's parents toss chestnuts and dates at the bride—a wish for many children—and she tries to catch them in her large skirt. The *p'ye-baek* ceremony continues with the other members of the groom's family, until the bride has been properly introduced to all.

Korean-Americans often hold the *p'ye-baek* toward the end of the reception, when many of the guests have left. It is usually a family-only affair, hosted by the groom's side. Family members try to say something profound as they are served tea, and the younger members often return the bride's bow. Gifts of money in white envelopes are also offered to the bride.

East and West: The Japanese Wedding Ceremony

In ancient Japanese myth, as mentioned before, all things were created by the marriage of the male and female ancestral gods, Izanagi and Izanami. In the spring, the Japanese hold festivals throughout the country celebrating their marriage. And in agricultural communities, marriages are a sign of an abundant harvest, a fertility rite that the whole village shares.

Today's traditional Shinto ceremony was first held in 1900 for the crown prince who later became Taisho Emperor, and was set in stone by an imperial marriage decree. Before this became a national ritual, every class of society held its own style of ceremony, mixing cultural and religious influences in a particular way. The royal ceremony, however, has at its roots ancient traditions common to all people and classes of Japan.

Shintoism is an age-old belief indigenous to Japan's shores. Also called *kami no michi*, or "way of the *kami*," it worships *kami*, the spirits inherent in the natural world. Shinto celebrations are very much a celebration of life itself, for it is believed the spirits of the mountains, the harvest, the village, the ancestors play important roles in people's daily lives.

The Shinto wedding ceremony embodies many rituals common to other Shinto services: a purification by the priest, an invocation and prayer to the *kami,* and an offering of food and drink to them. The ceremony begins with the purification of all participants and their guests, and the area. The bridal couple sit before the sanctuary, the go-betweens behind them and their families in two rows facing each other. After a short prayer, the priest picks up a special branch used for purification, the *harai-gushi,* and waves it around the room. He then chants the invocation, or *norito,* calling to the gods, Izanagi and Izanami among them, to bless the couple.

The next step is the ritual sharing of sake, or *sakazukigoto.* More secular than religious, the sharing of sake is one of the oldest elements of the ceremony, dating back to the time when sharing a sip of sake was as formal a bond as a Victorian handshake. Bride and groom drink from each of three flat sake cups stacked on top of one another, taking three sips. The order in which they drink may vary from village to village. The groom usually leads, taking three sips from the first cup. The bride is then offered the same cup, and also

The Chinese wedding procession was a parade of colors and sounds, peopled by attendants, lantern and banner bearers, gong beaters, and other musicians. Highlighting it was the passage of the bride in an ornate sedan chair. Green bamboo, symbolizing her purity, supported the sedan chair; if the bamboo was young enough to still have leaves, it was said the bride's family would live long lives.

takes three sips. They move on to the second and then the third cups. The ritual is popularly called *san-san-kudo: san* means "three," *ku* means "nine," *do* is "deliver"—three sets of three sips equals nine.

The sake is then offered to the couple's families, first the

groom's father, then the groom's mother, the bride's father, and the bride's mother. Finally, with the go-between, the entire group shares sake, to underline the joining of the two families. (In more modern ceremonies, the couple may exchange rings at this time, or wait until later.) All participants stand as the groom recites the vows of trust and affection—usually written by the priests at the shrine—before the altar. He speaks on behalf of the couple; the bride adds her name at the end of the vow. One Japanese-American couple, in deference to this personal vow, read love letters to their families at the reception.

In the final ritual, husband and wife turn to the altar and offer the *tamagushi,* a green branch from the sacred *sakaki* tree with strips of white paper attached. They turn its base first toward their bodies, then toward the altar, and place the *tamagushi* at the sanctuary, a gift for the *kami.* A last prayer, and the priest offers his congratulations to the couple.

Japanese-Americans, strangely enough, have not, in large numbers, carried the Shinto wedding traditions to these shores. Many Japanese-Americans seeking ties to their heritage marry in Buddhist churches and follow Buddhist traditions. The reasons are not clear. The Reverend George Matsubayashi, head of the Venice Hongwanji Buddhist Temple in the Los Angeles area for thirty years, explains that in Japan, the population follows the traditions of both Shintoism and Buddhism. There, however, Shintoism is reserved for living celebrations such as weddings, and Buddhism, with its emphasis on ancestral worship, is for funerals.

In the United States, a more religious society than Japan, many Japanese-Americans prefer the more spiritual, doctrinal aspects of Buddhism, Matsubayashi explains. Another reason many Japanese-Americans marry in Buddhist churches may be that there are many more Buddhist churches than Shinto shrines. There are roughly ten Shinto shrines in the country, all located on the West Coast. The Reverend Alfred Tsuyuki of the Konko Church in Los Angeles says he frequently travels across the country to perform weddings for Japanese-Americans interested in a Shinto service.

In the Reverend Matsubayashi's church, one of sixty-one members of the Buddhist Churches of America (just one sect of Buddhism), the ceremony is adopted from Buddhist scriptures. In Buddhist belief, individuals do not marry individuals. Rather, the individual pledges his or her devotion to the greater Truth. Individuals, explains the Reverend Matsubayashi, are flawed, and a marriage based on flaws may not last. But one based on Truth will be eternal.

After the couple walks down the aisle, the Reverend Matsubayashi hands them a rosary, or *o juju.* There are twenty-one beads, of two different colors, on the rosary. Eighteen beads represent the couple, two represent each family, and one represents the Buddha. The beads, tied on one string, symbolize the joining of the families, and the realization that no one is alone in this life. The bride and groom use the *o juju* as they offer incense and prayers to Amida Buddha.

After the prayers, the Reverend Matsubayashi explains in his sermon the meaning of the rosary. The couple then offer their vows, with the Buddha as witness. The wedding vows end with these words, the three treasures: "I put my faith in Buddha. I put my faith in Dharma [the Buddha's teachings]. I put my faith in Sangha [the religious order or brotherhood]. *Namu-Amida-Butsu* [I place myself in Amida Buddha]."

At the conclusion of the vows, the participants perform the *san-san-kudo*. The Reverend Matsubayashi separates the sharing of sake from the formal vows because he feels the tradition is secular, not religious. Yet his beautiful interpretation of the ritual has strong Buddhist sentiment. The first *san,* he says, stands for the three couples: the bride and groom, and both sets of parents. The second *san* represents the three "human delusions" or failings: passion, hatred, and ignorance. *Ku,* or nine, is a number of great potential, the last single digit before the sequence turns to double digits. *Do,* to deliver, is the couple's dedication to rid their lives of those human failings. The exchange of sake unifies all three couples in this quest.

After the exchange of sake, the Reverend Matsubayashi speaks about the importance of parents and asks the couple to thank their parents for everything they've done. The couple then turn to their parents to hug them and perhaps offer flowers. With this circle complete, the ceremony ends.

Five Rituals:
The Chinese Wedding Ceremony

In the late afternoon on the day of the wedding, the groom's representatives, accompanied by a parade of the matchmaker, musicians, banner carriers, lantern holders, gong beaters, brothers of the groom, and other attendants bearing gifts, a letter of welcome, and a sedan chair, fetch the bride from her parents' home; this is the first of the day's five rituals. Before she leaves, she says good-bye to the family gods and ancestors, and honors her parents and other elders by serving them tea. With her red veil in place, and to the clanging of gongs, she rushes for the sedan chair. It is believed that if she lingers too long at her doorstep, her good energy will remain inside and the wealth of her family will escape out the door. An umbrella or a rice basket is held over her head by her attendants as she enters the sedan chair. In its shadow, she is shielded from the heaven's eyes, safe from any wayward god who may do her harm while she is in this vulnerable state between the protection of her own family and that of her husband's.

In her hands the bride holds an apple, a symbol of the peace and tranquility she brings from her home, and a fan that she tosses from the sedan chair to show she will never return home. As the procession winds its way through town, she also throws out winter melon candies, symbolic of her bad habits.

When the procession arrives at the groom's home for the second ritual, it is met by the loud hiss and boom of firecrackers, to scare off evil spirits. The sedan chair is passed over a pot of charcoal to burn away any evil spirits that may be traveling with the bride. For further assurance, the groom shoots three pointless arrows into the sky to chase off any mischievous ghosts. Apple in hand, the bride steps off the sedan chair and walks over a saddle, another symbol of peace and tranquility. She is greeted by a young boy who presents her with a tangerine, a symbol of good fortune. An elderly woman whose life has been full of luck escorts her to the reception room, where she will await the groom.

When he arrives, bride and groom together bow three times at the altar of the gods of heaven and earth. The decorated altar is laden with offerings—a roast pig, ducks, chickens—incense and candles. Kneeling before it on a red cloth, the groom lifts the veil from the bride's face. (In traditional times, this might have been his first glimpse of his bride.) They both then sip wine from delicate nuptial cups, which are tied together with red string. Sometimes, as was done in high-class weddings in the Sung dynasty, the bride and groom themselves are tied together with a red sash. Crossing arms, they exchange cups and drink again. This is the essence of the third ritual, *tuan yuan,* "completing the circle." The sharing and mingling of wine means that their married life will be harmonious.

The fourth ritual is the honoring of the groom's ancestors at the family altar. Here, the bride presents mock paper money, and shoes, clothes, and hats to the ancestors. In the Sung dynasty, a master of ceremonies might present the bride to the ancestors with this prayer:

> May the bride bow to the gods of heaven and
> earth, the King Father of the East, and the Queen
> Mother of the West.
> May the bride bow to the taboo dragon spirit of
> the family and to the well, stove, and gate guardians.
> May the bride bow to all of the spirits served with
> incense in this house.
> May the bride bow to the great-great-grandfather,
> the great-grandfather and great-grandmother, the
> grandfather and grandmother.
> May the bride bow to all of the seniors among the
> agnatic and affinal relatives of her parents-in-law.
> Today, your great-grandson dares to report to you,

along with all the spirits in the ancestral temple: Senior grandson has taken the daughter of _____ family as his wife. This morning, they have performed the great coming home. We dare to introduce her according to ritual, with respect and reverence. Please enjoy these offerings.

After the prayers, more firecrackers are set off to signal the end of the formal ceremony. The bride and groom retire to their wedding chamber, which is bedecked in red satin for luck. Here, they offer prayers to the gods of the bedroom, the gods of children, and to each other. The master of ceremonies may scatter grains, money, fruit, or candies on the bed—again, a wish for many children—as the prayers are being said.

The bride's final duty of this wedding day is to serve tea to her new in-laws; the traditional tea ceremony, or *cha tao,* is held at many major life events. In the main room, a table set with symbolic offerings—oranges for luck; sticky cake, or *gao,* for a sweet life; and candied fruits for prosperity and longevity—is placed in a prominent location. Starting with the oldest and moving down the line to the youngest, the bride, bowing or kneeling, serves a cup of sweet tea with a lotus seed to each member of the groom's family, calling each person by his or her formal title. After each has drunk the tea, the bride collects the cup and receives in return a gift of money in the *hung bao,* a lucky red envelope, or jewelry.

Many Asian-Americans bring tradition to their wedding ceremonies, either in public or in private. Here in America, all too many of us hurry through our ceremonies, uncomfortable with ritual, religion, and emotion. Adding even more ceremony to your day may seem superfluous. But wedding ceremonies, whether modern or traditional, offer ways to express in simple gestures some of the intense feelings flowing through you, your family, and your guests. Your vows before each other, before your families and friends, and before a higher presence show your respect for all. In return, there is the unspoken promise from your family and friends and your God that they will help protect and nurture your marriage.

As our ancestors knew, wedding ceremonies are as much about family and community and duty to a higher being as they are about today's notion of romantic love between individuals. Like the mingling of sweet wine in a homemade gourd, the marriage of these two ideals, one ancient and one modern, can produce a joyous union that will last forever.

PART III

Completing the Circle

Chapter Eight

SOLEMN SPEECHES AND
SEXY GAMES:
THE RECEPTION

*At Katushika the river water
Runs gently, and the plum blossom
Bursts out laughing.
The nightingale cannot withstand so many joys
And sings, and we are reconciled.
Our warm bodies touch,
Cane branch and pine branch.*

—JAPANESE LOVE SONG

WEDDING RECEPTIONS are celebrations. For most people, the day's solemnity is over and the festivities can get under way. For the Japanese, however, there is more to a reception than just food and fun. After the bride and groom emerge from the intimate Shinto wedding ceremony and are announced to their waiting guests, the speeches—some formal, some funny—begin.

The first to lay claim to the microphone is the *nakodo.* The go-between

The mandarin ducks, intertwined,
   become a pair.
It is time to have the good dream
   of a bear
And see pearls fall into your hands.

Couples married during China's Sung dynasty may have heard this ode on their wedding day. The ducks symbolized love and fidelity. Dreams of bears were said to portend the birth of sons, and pearls represented pregnancy.

formally introduces the bride and groom to the guests, giving their dates of birth, their school histories, their occupations, hobbies, and honors, and even describing their temperaments and work habits. He proclaims the excellence of the match—remember, the *nakodo*'s name is staked to the couple's success—to the gathered family and friends. In closing remarks, the *nakodo* traditionally appeals to listeners to support the couple throughout their marriage.

After the *nakodo,* one or more *shuhin* rise to say a few words on behalf of the assembled guests. This "principal guest" could be a boss of the bride or groom, a former teacher, or another distinguished guest. Like the *nakodo,* the *shuhin* praises the couple's character and work habits. The *shuhin* might also offer words of advice, warnings about possible tempests ahead, and reflections on the ideal marriage.

Throughout the rest of the reception, congratulatory speeches called *shukuji* are offered by older guests and young friends of the couple. The more formal are made by company superiors, friends of the families, and former teachers. These usually mirror the remarks made by the *nakodo* and the *shuhin.* As the reception progresses, the younger friends become less formal—the generous quantities of sake offered at weddings help—roasting the bride or groom by telling funny, embarrassing, and sometimes ribald stories. One note: Speakers take great pains to avoid saying words like *kireru,* which means "to cut," or "to be broken" and *hanareru* or *wakareru,* which mean "to separate."

Japanese-Americans often continue the tradition of wedding speeches; close family members, professors, and colleagues are asked to say a few words about the couple. One couple turned the tables: They read specially written letters to family and friends at their reception, a heartfelt interpretation of the custom. Here, the tradition was more friendly than formal, the words adding a personal touch. In Japan, speeches have another purpose: to promote marriage and societal ideals. The emphasis on the "hardworking groom," "cheerful bride," household harmony, new responsibilities of marriage, and the happiness and approval of the parents reinforces society's expectations of young married people.

On the lighter side, guests at Japanese weddings are encouraged to offer some kind of entertainment. It may be a dance or a short musical performance, a reading of a poem or classical literature. Karaoke is also popular. At some weddings, guests are allowed to tease the bride and groom into revealing secret details of their relationship. In one popular game, the wedding hall director conducts a mock interview with them. They answer potentially embarrassing *Newlywed Game*-style questions, such as, "When did you first kiss?"

Chinese brides and grooms also fall prey to their more gregarious guests. After the sumptuous banquet is over, the merrymakers follow the couple into their bedroom. There, with off-color jokes and suggestive banter, they cajole the bride and groom into playing erotic games for their entertainment; the ancient practice is known as "warming up the bedchamber." By custom, guests are allowed to stay with the couple for three successive days and nights. It is believed that fox spirits, who can sometimes appear in the guise of seductive women, are jealous of newlyweds and could harm the innocent couple. A loud crowd of revelers would frighten away these evil demons, and so the guests are encouraged to stay.

The games can get pretty suggestive. In one, the guests scatter beans over the bride's body, and make the groom pick them off with his mouth. In another, the groom thrusts his hand under the bride's clothes and gives a running commentary of what he finds. In another game, "drinking from the flesh cup," a mouthful of wine sipped by the groom must be transferred to the bride's mouth.

In the nineteenth century in the United States and Europe, guests might accompany the new couple into their bedroom, drinking and singing bawdy songs until the wee hours of the morning. Korean villagers today are more subtle. The couple is left alone, but the unmarried women of the village are invited to spy on them their first night. They poke holes through the paper and bamboo screens, and may "visit" the couple at any time. The holes these silent

Soaking with flowing tears our
sleeve,
We vowed that we should love
on still,
Though waves rise and no traces
leave
Of our love-trysting pine-clad hill.

Chigiriki na katami ni sode
wo shibori tsutsu
Sue no matsu yama nami
kosaji to wa

—Kiyowara-no Motosuke,
from *One Hundred Poems*
from One Hundred Poets
(thirteenth-century Japan)

voyeurs create have another purpose: they serve as exits for the evil spirits who may also be watching the couple.

Reds, Golds, and Greens: Festive Decorations

Your reception can be held in virtually any place that tickles your fancy. Our Asian ancestors traditionally held the wedding banquet in the courtyard of a home, a sentimental place to have a reception. Intimate locations may be available at a price: a local landmark house, a museum garden, a beach hideaway. For many Asian-Americans, however, space—and lots of it—is important. Weddings are a major event: with the emphasis placed on family, don't be surprised if many of your extended family members make the trip from the far reaches of China and Korea. For the Japanese, the extra dignitaries—bosses and teachers, old faces and new—can run up the guest list as well. (In Japan, however, weddings are so expensive that only fifty to one hundred guests are the norm.) With this in mind, some larger Asian restaurants have private halls for eight hundred guests or more.

Whatever the space, whether it's a tent at your home or a private room at the country club, there are many ways to inject your heritage. The bright red banners of Chinese celebrations, emblazoned with the distinctive "double happiness" character, can enliven any room. More subtle tasteful red lanterns can grace tables or corners. Red tablecloths or red flowers can provide a festive air, as can the golden images of the wondrous phoenix and benevolent dragon, the traditional symbol of bride and groom. For an unusual centerpiece, what about a pair of goldfish in a crystal bowl? In place of a guest book, the Chinese have guests sign a piece of red or pink silk embroidered with the character for "double happiness." Placed on a table in an entranceway, the cloth will be a unique, lasting memory of your day.

For Korean-Americans, beautiful screens with images of peonies, birds, and flowers can bring the wonders of the garden indoors. Screens were an integral part of any Korean household, adding a feeling of luxury and abundance, even in the coldest winter.

Family crests are a popular motif for 1,001 origami crane displays. These two crests, each constructed of the 1,001 tiny paper cranes, could be shown at a wedding reception. The cranes, which symbolize good wishes, can also be mounted as Chinese characters, animals, even cars.

As mentioned before, wedding ceremonies are traditionally performed in front of a screen painted with peonies, a harbinger of
good fortune. Screens with paintings of birds, animals, and flowers
have their own symbolism. Pairs of animals represent the Taoist concept of yin and yang, male and female. The image of jumping carp,
a fish associated with courage, is a wish for a strong son; a woman
who dreamed of a jumping carp, it was thought, would give birth to
a son who would see success in his life. Pictures of wild geese and
mandarin ducks, which mate for life, are wishes for marital fidelity.

At the Palisadium, a popular place for wedding receptions
among Korean-Americans in Fort Lee, New Jersey, decorative
screens can be borrowed for the wedding ceremony. If you're not
holding your reception there, ask to rent one at your local Korean
store, or borrow one from your relatives.

Like the goose, the elegant snow-white crane, favored by
the Japanese, takes only one mate in life and is often pictured with
the pine tree as a symbol of a long, contented married life. To honor
this loyal bird, many Japanese-Americans fold 1,001 cranes origami-
style to decorate their wedding halls. Why 1,001? Asians are fond of
hyperbole. The exaggerated number means good luck a thousand

How to Fold an Origami Crane

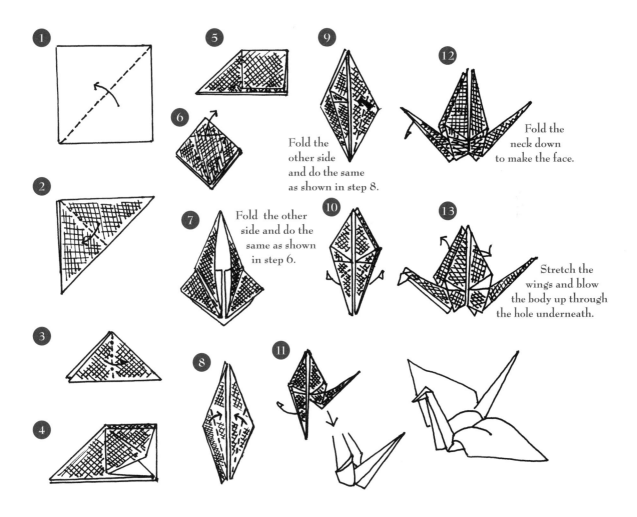

5

6

9 Fold the other side and do the same as shown in step 8.

12 Fold the neck down to make the face.

2

7 Fold the other side and do the same as shown in step 6.

10

13 Stretch the wings and blow the body up through the hole underneath.

3

8

11

4

times over and then some. The cranes, created from colorful and delicate paper, are scattered over the tables at the reception, used to adorn the cake table, or perhaps balanced on wine and water glasses. Some Japanese-Americans, especially on the West Coast, use gold and silver foil cranes to form shapes such as the characters *konji,* long life, and *kotobuki,* good luck, or family crests; these are lovely

HAN FENG
ON DECORATING
THE RECEPTION HALL

HAN FENG, a native of China known for her ready-to-wear collections carried by such stores as Saks Fifth Avenue and Henri Bendel, had an all-Western wedding, because, she says, that's what she wanted at the time. She even borrowed her wedding gown from her mother-in-law's neighbor, a creation from the fifties.

But if she could do it again, she would make it more Chinese. She would wear the traditional Chinese dress and serve a mixture of Chinese and Western foods. As for decorations, she says, "I would make everything red. I love the color. The Chinese believe it is the color of luck. I would design the whole room in it—red flowers, red tablecloths, red napkins, red curtains, and red lanterns on the table."

souvenirs of the day. A Japanese-American bride and Chinese-American groom combined their cultures in a thoughtful way: she folded 1,001 cranes and had them arranged to spell out her groom's Chinese name.

The delicate butterfly, considered by Japanese, Chinese, and Korean cultures as a symbol of lasting married love, can also add tradition to decorations. The Koreans use butterflies to adorn screens; the Japanese use bows to suggest the shape of the butterfly.

Whereas in the West butterflies are considered fragile and

TOM UYENO
ON DECORATING
WITH FLOWERS

To CREATE an Asian look at a reception, the Japanese–American florist Tom Uyeno, who has created flower arrangements for such television shows as *General Hospital* and *Days of Our Lives,* consults his heritage. For the tables, Uyeno makes ikebana-style centerpieces, using low, round vases for his graceful creations. Ikebana, Japanese flower arrangement, is a high art form. Masters train for years perfecting the right balance of heaven, earth, and humanity. Uyeno takes his hint from the seasons, relying on such flowers as chrysanthemums in fall and cherry blossoms in spring.

For the head table, Uyeno does something special. He may string garlands topped with flowers around the table. If there's room, he may create a miniature Japanese garden behind the couple, with plum trees and their exquisite blossoms, small brush pines, and flowering plants.

At the entrance to the reception hall, Uyeno places more delicate flowering trees and small brush pine, bamboo, even a Japanese stone lantern, so "guests feel they've entered a garden."

symbolize life's brevity, the East treasures them as symbols of long life. The Chinese word for "butterfly," *tieh,* sounds like a word meaning "seventy or eighty years old." Tales of the magical charms of the butterfly abound. In one, told by the Taoist philosopher Chuang-tzu, a student follows a beautiful butterfly into the private garden of a retired magistrate. There he catches a glimpse of the magistrate's lovely daughter. The student redoubles his efforts to become successful, determined to win her hand. The butterfly cupid does not fail, and the student not only marries the magistrate's daughter but also becomes a high-ranking official.

Japanese mythology tells another tale of unending love involving the butterfly. An elderly bachelor, a recluse most of his life, falls ill one day. Fearing his illness might be his last, he invites his widowed sister-in-law and her son to come care for him in his final days. One day, while the nephew is watching his uncle sleeping, an enormous white butterfly flies into the room and settles on his pillow. The nephew tries to brush it off, but it remains, fluttering and circling above the uncle's bed. The nephew chases the butterfly from room to room but it keeps hovering. Suddenly, in one decisive swoop, it heads out the window. His uncle still asleep, the boy follows the butterfly to discover its origins. Strangely, it flies to the nearby cemetery and disappears into an old but well-tended grave with the name Akiko on the tombstone. The nephew returns home. In the few minutes he has been away, his uncle has died.

After the funeral, the boy describes the odd behavior of the butterfly to his mother. She explains that when his uncle was young, he was engaged to a girl named Akiko. They were deeply in love, but sadly, Akiko died shortly before they were to be married. In mourning, the uncle bought a home close to her grave site and, for fifty years, tended the tomb with love and care. No doubt, the boy's mother says, the haunting white butterfly was Akiko's spirit come to fetch the soul of the man she loved.

Ceremonial Rituals at the Reception

One way to celebrate your heritage is by holding all or part of the traditional wedding ceremony at the reception. My husband and I performed the Chinese tea ceremony at our reception, to introduce ourselves formally to our new families. We kept our Western attire; others honor their heritage by changing into colorful traditional clothes. We weren't sure what our friends would make of the rite, the third wedding ritual of a very hot day. To our delight, the tea ceremony was moving and memorable for all.

At a reception site, which may not be set up with religious altars or artifacts, secular rituals may be more appropriate than the religious ones. For example, Japanese–American couples may wish to skip the Shinto purification rituals and sip sake in the *san-san-kudo.* A change of costume to the colorful *furisode*—one way the Japanese bride signals a less formal atmosphere at the reception—might highlight the ceremony. Korean–American couples can honor their families by performing the *p'ye-baek,* the introduction ceremony. They may even play a few games: in one, the groom lifts the bride onto his back—symbolizing his new "burden"—and trots her around the room. Chinese-Americans might pin traditional red name tags on the tea ceremony participants; the red emblems with their gold characters emphasize the authenticity of the rite.

Bring these ancient ceremonies to life by playing traditional music in the background. Or add drama with dance. One couple hired a troupe that performed with two "lions," clanging gongs, and drums. A Japanese *od-dio* dancer graced another reception.

To make the experience more meaningful for your guests, ask a friend or relative to play emcee. Family members may need to be introduced, and someone may need to explain the significance of, for instance, the *san-san-kudo* cup or the throwing of dates and chestnuts. Be sure the symbolism of your costume's brilliant colors, the embroidery, makeup, or headdress is explained. If you don't want a running play-by-play, include an explanation in your wedding program, or place the information on each table.

Finally, you may want to include your guests in this special moment. Ask them to join you in the last sip of sake, or bow to

Shugi-bukuro, *envelopes decorated with gold and silver strings that are, symbolically, impossible to untie, are used at many ceremonial events to give cash—a very acceptable gift in Japan. Guests must be quite generous in their wedding gifts: for a friend, the equivalent of $300 is the norm; for a close friend, the figure is around $500; and if the bride or groom is an employee, nephew, or niece, the amount may top $1,000. It's hard to be cheap: the amount of cash given is written on the outside of the envelope, along with the giver's name.*

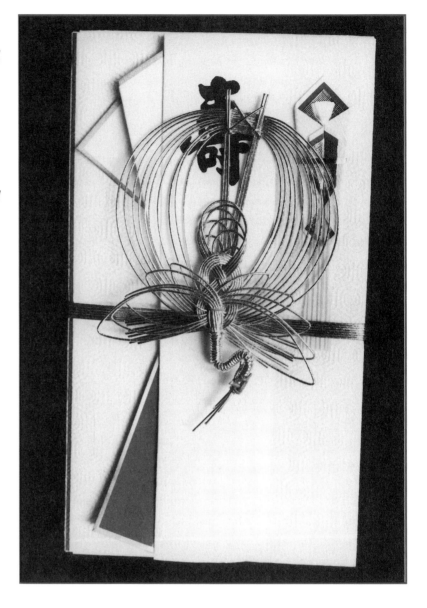

them when the tea ceremony is over. They can even join in the fun of throwing dates and chestnuts into your skirt, if bowls of them are on the tables.

Honoring Your Guests: Salutes and Gifts

In Asia, the guest is extremely important and holds a position of high respect; great care is taken to assure a guest's comfort and happiness. At home, a guest may be showered with offerings of food and drink. At weddings, guests are entertained like royalty. It is a matter of face; this is no time to be stingy. During the reception, the couple and their parents visit each table to greet the guests and receive their congratulations and toasts. More important during these rounds are the families' fervent thanks to the guests for honoring them at this occasion. In modern Japan, the couple light a candle symbolically at each table, sharing their warmth with the gathered family and friends.

Your guests may also appreciate a small gift from your wedding, something they can take away and treasure. In Japan, brides and grooms spend an average of thirty to fifty dollars on these gifts, or *hikidemono,* sometimes much more. They may give a set of dishes, a crystal vase, or a bag of sweets. *Kohaku manjyu,* a round steamed bun with sweet bean paste in the middle, is another popular gift. A pair of buns, one red, one white, both larger than usual, are presented to guests in a special box.

Even simpler gifts may suffice. One couple placed a beautiful pair of chopsticks at each place setting, tied with a ribbon imprinted with their names and the wedding date. Another gave out special fortune cookies with a message of thanks. A handful of origami cranes, a lace bag of candied almonds, a bamboo box of dates and chestnuts offered with the wedding cake or pressed into a guest's hand on parting may be appropriate.

Again, the message of love is clear though unspoken. The Chinese-American fashion designer Han Feng says it best. If she had to do her wedding over again, she would make sure each guest received a gift. "The guests bring so much luck and good wishes with them. I want to share my love with them in return."

Chapter Nine

THE WEDDING BANQUET

E AT WELL, drink well, and be healthy for a long, happy life," goes the Chinese saying. Nowhere is this advice followed more than at the wedding banquet, where course upon course of mouth-watering delicacies and tantalizing treats are lavished on guests. Food has always been of prime importance to Asian cultures, its tempting tastes and elegant preparation the highest gift one can offer. Every major celebration revolves around food.

There is an enticing harmony at an Asian table. Cold foods are balanced with hot, salty with sweet, boiled with fried. The colors of ingredients are noted— a traditional meal must be as pleasing to the eye as it is to the palate. Color is cherished also for its symbolism. Red foods such as lobster are served at Chinese and Japanese

POSSAM KIMCHI
(WRAPPED-UP KIMCHI)

You may want to reduce the amount of red pepper powder in this side dish to accommodate your less courageous guests.

1 head Chinese cabbage
1 carrot
1 Korean white radish
¼ pear
2 stone mushrooms
2 dried brown oak mushrooms
½ bunch watercress
3 water chestnuts
½ octopus
1 green onion
2 cloves garlic
1 knob ginger
2 ounces oysters
2 tablespoons salted anchovies
½ cup red pepper powder
2 tablespoons salted shrimp juice
1 cup coarse salt
1 tablespoon sugar
Red pepper threads
1 teaspoon pine nuts

1. Remove outer leaves from cabbage and halve it lengthwise. Soak in salted water and let stand for 6 hours.
2. Cut carrot, radish, and pear into 1-by-1¼-inch squares, ¼ inch thick.

weddings for their lucky presence. Other foods as well are symbolic wishes—fish for abundance, chestnuts for many children, noodles for long life. The Asian banquet is a feast for the eyes, mind, and heart, not just for the belly.

Many Asian-Americans host a traditional wedding banquet. Chinese-Americans are the most likely to serve ethnic foods, maybe because theirs are easier to find in this country. Japanese-Americans seem the least likely to feast on their traditional dishes—American or continental foods are more trendy for this set. But even if Asian-Americans do not serve the elaborate banquets of the past, many still include one or more traditional dishes—for example, the Korean sticky rice cake, *dok,* or lotus seed soup.

Ask your caterer or banquet manager if any Asian dishes can be prepared. With ethnic foods becoming more mainstream, you may be surprised by how well the kitchen can accommodate you. Or you may want to order special foods from an outside shop to supplement a Western menu. An older auntie (or uncle) also might be willing to prepare a traditional dish for the day.

The wedding dishes listed here are just a sampling of the many symbolic foods you might serve. Wedding foods vary from region to region. Wedding feasts differ, for example, among the four major food regions of China, Canton in the south, Szechuan in the west, Mandarin in the north, and Shanghai in the east. Each region has its own delicacies, as do Chinese settlements outside the mainland, in such places as Malaysia, Burma, Hong Kong, and the Philippines. Most major Chinese restaurants in the United States are Cantonese—the southern Chinese were the first to immigrate and establish themselves in this country—though other Chinese varieties are gaining in popularity.

Use the ingredients, menus, and recipes given here as a guide to your own gastronomic feast. You don't need to limit these treats to your wedding banquet: serve them at your engagement party, shower, or rehearsal dinner too. Whatever your traditions, food—and lots of it—should be a memorable part of your wedding.

Iwaizen:
The Japanese Wedding Banquet

Every dish in the Japanese wedding banquet is a wish—for happiness, prosperity, long life, or many children. The symbolism may lie in the name of the food, which might sound like another word. For example, *konbu*, or kelp, is often served because the word sounds like the last half of the word for "joy," *yorokobu*. Or the wishes may be hidden in how the food is prepared. *Tai*, sea bream, is often served whole, its head and tail forced up from the plate so the fish almost forms a circle—the Zen symbol of eternity. The shape of the food or the dish in which it is served also have meanings: cucumbers cut in the shape of fans garnish some dishes, the fan signifying a bright future. Finally, the color of the food may also speak of good wishes, red, for instance, being the color of luck.

A traditional wedding meal might have the following foods, cooked in a variety of ways—grilled, deep-fried, boiled, or raw.

- Red tuna and white *tai* (sea bream). Red and white are the colors of celebration, and *tai* recalls the word for "lucky."

- Clams. Clams are served with both shells together, the two halves symbolizing the happy couple.

- Salted herring roe. The eggs are a symbol of many children.

- Lobster. Lobster, *ise-ebi*, is offered for a number of reasons. First for its red color. Served bent backward, it also symbolizes long life. In addition, this crustacean stands for prayer, as *ise* brings to mind the Ise shrine, the oldest Shinto shrine in Japan. Traditionally, the

3. Soak mushrooms in water until soft and clean. Cut into thin strips.

4. Remove roots and leaves from watercress and cut stems into 1¼-inch pieces. Slice water chestnuts into flat pieces.

5. Clean octopus by rubbing with salt, rinse with cold water, and cut into 1¼-inch pieces. Cut green onion, garlic, and ginger into thin strips.

6. Wash salted cabbage and drain. Save salted water for later use. Cut stem area into 2¼-inch pieces. Place stem pieces on outer leaves and wrap them temporarily.

7. Mix ingredients from steps 2 through 5, oysters and anchovies with red pepper powder. Season with salted shrimp juice, salt, and sugar. Add red pepper threads and pine nuts, and mix well. This is the stuffing.

8. Pack stuffing around each stem piece and wrap pieces firmly in outer cabbage leaves.

9. Put wrapped bundles one by one in a crock, pour reserved salted water over them, and weigh them down with a heavy stone.

 (From Noh Chin-hwa, *Traditional Korean Cooking*)

THE DRINK OF THE GODS

SAKE, LITERALLY the "drink of the gods," is made from rice that has been steamed and fermented and then mixed with water. The best sake comes from just a few areas of Japan: Nada, Akita, Hiroshima, and Fushimi. True connoisseurs prefer *junmaishu*, pure sake without added sugar or alcohol. For the rest of us, there are three grades: *tokkyu* (special), *ikkyu* (first-grade), and *nikkyu* (second-grade).

Drink sake while it's young—three months at best, no older than a year. *Kanpai!*

lobster is served without claws: claws cut—not an appropriate concept for a happy event.

- *Konbu* (kelp). This special seaweed is used as an ingredient or a garnish, as noted above. It may be tied in the shape of bamboo, a festive symbol.

- Abalone. At New Year's time, abalone, a symbol of long life, is dried and pounded paper-thin. At weddings, it is often served raw.

- *Ume-boshi* (dried plum). Plums are festive symbols.

- *Kohaku manjyu*. These round red or white buns with sweet bean paste inside may be served at the banquet or given as gifts.

- Carrots, cucumbers, mashed yam, taro root. These can be molded and formed into shapes such as fans, cranes, and turtles. Cranes and

ORANGES FOR LUCK

THE CHINESE LOVE to end a heavy meal with a light serving of fruit, especially oranges. At weddings, this is especially appropriate: oranges symbolize good fortune. Sheila Lukins, coauthor of *The Silver Palate Cookbook,* offers this twist in her *All Around the World Cookbook*: Sprinkle cinnamon over peeled or sliced oranges. (Allow one orange per person, and don't forget to remove the pith, the bitter white part of the skin.) You might drizzle rose water over the orange before adding the cinnamon. Top off the dessert with scattered rose petals for a romantic look.

turtles are symbols for long life and happiness. The leaf of the nandina plant, *nanten,* is also used to decorate wedding dishes; the syllable *ten* recalls the word *tenjiru,* meaning "to challenge."

THE JAPANESE TABLE

The highest style of Japanese cooking is *kaiseki*. Consisting of as many as fifteen tiny dishes of no more than a mouthful, *kaiseki* began as accompaniment to the traditional tea ceremony. Each dish is a work of art; each must be appreciated with the eyes before it is enjoyed by the mouth. *Kaiseki* banquets follow a set order of courses: first appetizers, then a clear soup, then sashimi. A grilled dish is followed by a boiled one, a deep-fried one, a steamed one, and finally a salad. The meal ends with rice served with pickles and miso soup.

Whether a meal is served *kaiseki* or home style, the number of dishes count. The Japanese do not like the number four, *shi*, which sounds like the word for "death." So you may have a dinner with two soups and seven dishes or three soups and eleven dishes—but never a number of courses that is a multiple of four.

The wedding banquet is served in a special way. Strangely enough, only some of the *iwaizen* dishes—the soup and the sashimi, for example—are eaten at the wedding. The rest are packed in a box, the *okizume*, and taken home by guests. The chopsticks used for eating *iwaizen* are also unusual. While regular chopsticks are square-shaped and sharpened on one end, the special chopsticks are round and half-sharpened on both edges. The envelope for these chopsticks, *hashi-bukuro*, is made of red-and-white paper and tied with gold and silver strings, or *mizuhiki*.

Suggested Menus

TRADITIONAL
from Japan Inn, Washington, D.C.

KAISEKI

ZENSAI—ASSORTED APPETIZERS

Lobster *kogane-yaki:* Lobster and sea urchin
Sake hosho-yaki: Salmon
Komochi konbu: Herring roe on tangle, a type of kelp
Kohaku kamaboko: Red-and-white fishcake
Renkon amakara-ni: Japanese yam

SASHIMI—RAW

Maguro, hirame, amaebi: Tuna, flounder, sweet shrimp

NIMONO—SIMMERED

Imo, tako, nankin: Taro, octopus, squash

YAKIMONO—GRILLED
Tai: Red snapper

SUNOMONO—VINEGAR (SALAD)
Hamaguri, jiku-mitsuba, oroshi-ae: Clam, Japanese mint, radish

SHOKUJI—MAIN COURSE
Sekihan, misoshiru, konomono: Rice with red beans, miso soup, Japanese pickles

KUDAMONO—DESSERT
Melon

NOT-SO-TRADITIONAL
Wedding Luncheon, from Ellen Greaves, who has worked
at The Quilted Giraffe and March

Tomato consommé with daikon, *shizo,* and tiny peas
Soy mustard–glazed chicken on lightly pickled cucumber
Japanese rice with Chinese sausage and fermented black beans
Green-tea mousse

The Chinese Wedding Banquet

For the Chinese, a banquet is a way to show riches. Course after course of succulent meats, crispy vegetables, long noodles, and exotic delicacies emerges from the kitchen. There is usually so much food that guests are given red paper to wrap up the leftovers—unthinkable behavior at a Western reception. The more food, courses, and leftovers, the more generous and wealthy the hosts seem.

The hosts show their wealth also by the kinds of foods they offer. Bird's nest—a real nest made from the saliva and feathers of birds, and cooked in soup—is a cherished delicacy. The fewer feath-

1. Rub fish all over with salt and let stand for five minutes. (If fish is too wet, pat gently with paper towel first.) Rub fish with egg yolk, then coat with an even layer of cornstarch. Set aside.

2. Mix together onions, red pepper, and cucumber. Place half of mixture on serving dish.

3. Heat oil in a pan until very hot. Put fish in pan and turn heat down to medium. Deep-fry fish for 3 to 4 minutes, or until golden brown on each side. Place on serving dish.

4. Pour out all but 2 tablespoons oil. Brown shallot and ginger in oil. Prepare sauce mixture, add to pan, and bring to a boil. Add cornstarch solution and bring to a boil. Sprinkle remaining vegetables from step 2 on the fish and pour sauce over fish. Serve immediately.

 (From Sally Foo, Tanzania)

THE WEDDING CAKE

THE TRADITIONAL Western wedding cake, with its tiers of fluffy white frosting, has come to symbolize the wedding itself, coveted and copied by brides all over the world. In Japan, however, don't get too close: the cake may be made of rubber, with a slot for the knife. The real cake is back in the kitchen; this one's just for show.

Asians don't eat cake, at least as we know it in the West. In the East, desserts are made of gummy, sweetened rice or sweet beans. As an alternative, a Japanese-American bride might choose to cut and serve *yomogashima,* also called *komochi manjyu,* a very large *manjyu,* or sweet, round pastry with several smaller *manjyu* inside. The smaller *manjyu* have sweet bean-paste filling in five colors, symbolizing the wish for many children. One Japanese-American couple who had *komochi manjyu* for their wedding cake cut it with a red thread tied to their fingers, instead of a knife.

Japanese-American brides might serve slices of Western wedding cake with a small seasonal sweet, or *namagashi.* These sweets can be made in a variety of shapes, from birds to flowers. At Toraya in New York City, a branch of the famous 450-year-old Japanese bakery that has served emperors, more than 3,000 varieties of *namagashi* are offered.

ers the nest has, the more expensive it is. Various meats and seafoods are also prized for their extravagance.

And of course, Chinese foods have their special symbolism, usually traditional wishes for happiness, longevity, and many chil-

If you're looking to create a uniquely Asian-American wedding cake, Amy Ho, dessert chef at San Francisco's China Moon Cafe, has this suggestion: Since Asians don't like heavy cakes, she says, pick a lighter variety such as chiffon or sponge cake. Make it light-colored as well—Asians prefer lighter foods to darker ones. Layer the second tier with fruit such as mandarin oranges, sandwiched between butter cream frosting to prevent the juices from seeping through. (Don't put the fruit on the bottom layer; it needs to be strong enough to support the cake.)

These Japanese sweets, nama-gashi, can be made in a wide variety of forms, including birds and flowers. Serve them alongside your wedding cake for a special touch.

Frost the cake with a thin layer of white marzipan. Stay away from heavy butter cream frosting, which may be too sweet for Asian tastes, Ho says. Decorate the cake with fresh flowers to make it a feast for the eyes.

If you can't decide on your wedding cake, do as sumo wrestlers do. Instead of cutting a cake, they smash a barrel of sake with a hammer. Now *that* would be unique!

dren. A whole fish, *yu,* is always served: *yu* sounds like the word for "abundance"—a wish for a life without want.

The traditional banquet follows a set pattern. Foods are often served in fours: in China four is considered a lucky number.

KANPEI!

RAISING A GLASS to the bride and groom is a tradition—as well as a liability—on both sides of the Pacific. Chinese-American and Japanese-American brides and grooms are toasted as they move from table to table. The traditional toast is *Kanpei!* (Chinese) or *Kanpai!* (Japanese) meaning, literally, "dry glass." The most respectful way for the Chinese to toast is with both hands, one holding the top of the glass and one touching the bottom. Bottoms up, if you must. But just remember, you probably have many more tables ahead of you.

In Japan, it is considered impolite to fill your own glass, but polite to fill everybody else's. And don't forget the group cheer, *Banzai!* One guest stands and swiftly raises both hands, palms forward, above his head. *"Banzai!"* he shouts. As the group mimics the gesture and the toast, he repeats his *"Banzai!"* once, twice, three times.

The Koreans are more subtle. One shot of sake, *jung jong,* is imbibed just before the start of the meal, a quick, silent toast to the newlyweds.

There is also a yin–yang balance to the dishes served. And the meal shows off a range of cooking styles: stir-fried, steamed, deep-fried.

The wedding banquet often starts with a bang—the dragon-and-phoenix plate. Various cold foods including sliced meats, ham and chicken, delicacies such as abalone and jellyfish, and various kinds of nuts are shaped into a spectacular dragon and phoenix. This is followed by four types of hors d'oeuvres or by *dim sum*—dumplings are a popular choice. Four vegetable dishes and four light

SOO CHUNG KWA
(PERSIMMON PUNCH)
*Serve this sweet treat
as an exotic dessert.*

10 dried persimmons
2 tablespoons pine nuts
5½ ounces fresh ginger root
¼ ounce stick cinnamon
13 cups water
2 cups sugar

1. Remove seeds from persimmons and replace with four or five pine nuts.
2. Wash and scrape skin off ginger and slice thinly. Simmer ginger and cinnamon in water until it gives a fragrant smell. Add sugar and boil briefly.
3. Pour liquid through a fine sieve.
4. Pour syrup over dried persimmons in a large bowl.
5. When persimmons are soft, serve them with syrup and a sprinkle of pine nuts.

 (From Noh Chin-hwa, *Traditional Korean Cooking*)

vegetable-and-meat stir-fries come next, winding down the *xiao cao,* or "small dishes."

Then the main courses, the *ta cao,* or "big dishes," are served. Whole preparations are popular: whole chicken, whole duck, and definitely whole fish—fried, baked, or steamed. The wholeness is significant: nothing has been cut out (not even the head—this may cause squeamishness among Westerners). My favorite is Peking duck, a sweet-spiced duck prized for its crispy skin and served with Mandarin pancakes and tangy hoisin sauce. Pigeon is also served, its tender meat symbolizing peace. Lobster is offered for its color, as is red-stewed pork at Shanghai weddings.

Soups are a must. For wealthier families, rich shark's-fin soup is almost expected. The price is high: in some places, this silky yet crunchy delicacy can cost $150 per person! A noodle or rice dish rounds off the meal. When the noodles are boiled, care is taken not to break the noodles.

The Chinese don't customarily serve desserts, but at weddings often two—for the couple—are presented. Desserts are sweet, and so are a wish for sweet lives for the couple. One dessert is *lian zi,* lotus seeds cooked until soft and served with honey. The lotus seeds are a wish for many children. Another dessert is sweetened steamed bread, shaped and colored to resemble peaches, *tao zi*—another wish for long life.

Many Chinese-American hold their weddings in restaurants that have standard wedding menus from which to choose. You still may feel free to approach a manager and request a special dish.

One note: You might warn your Western guests of the overwhelming amount of food that will be offered by placing a menu on each table. The menu can explain the foods in each course, and perhaps something of their meanings. You might also tell guests that traditional banquets are served "family style," with the dishes placed in the middle of the table. Provide forks for the chopstick novices—or they may not get any food at all!

Suggested Menus

TRADITIONAL
from Shun Lee, New York City

Dragon-and-phoenix delicacies
Braised royal shark's fin
Roast squab with frog legs
Honey-glazed ham
Dungeness crab with black beans
Whole winter melon soup
Peking duck
Sea cucumber with shrimp roe
Sea turtle with rock candy
Vegetable delight
Fried rice with ham and shrimp
Double-delight dessert

NOT-SO-TRADITIONAL
from A Dish of Salt, New York City

BUTLERED HORS D'OEUVRES
Coconut prawn, crisp shrimp cake, honey shrimp ball, spring roll,
sesame beef roll, satay beef on skewer, barbecued spare rib,
steamed dumpling, curry beef dumpling

DINNER
Appetizer: Suckling pig, jellyfish, shrimp salad
with fresh fruit, roast pork
Individual yam basket of sautéed lobster, scallop, and shrimp
Seafood soup with winter melon
Phoenix chicken
Filet mignon with cremini mushrooms
Cantonese lobster

and let stand until cut sides are dry (but not hard) to the touch, 1 to 2 hours. Or dry slices by putting on a baking sheet in a 200°F oven until tops feel dry, about 15 minutes. Turn slices to dry undersides. (Dry bread will not absorb oil when fried.) Cooled toasts may be kept overnight in an airtight container.

2. Combine ginger, scallion, coriander, salt, wine, chili sauce, and pepper in a food processor. Add fish paste and puree. Transfer to a bowl and stir in water chestnuts. (Puree may be sealed and refrigerated overnight; press plastic wrap directly on surface of puree.)

3. Several hours before serving, complete fish mixture and ready toasts for frying: Whisk egg whites until stiff; fold into puree. Using a small spatula glazed with oil to keep fish paste from sticking, mound 2 tablespoons puree on each bread toast. Smooth puree into a plateau ½ inch thick, with sloping sides to meet toast, and no holes for oil to enter while frying. Put mounded toasts on a baking sheet. If working in advance, cover toasts loosely and refrigerate.

4. About 20 minutes before serving, pour 2 to 2½ inches

oil into a wok or large, deep, heavy skillet. Rest a deep-fry thermometer on rim and bring oil to the medium-haze stage, 375°F, hot enough to foam a dab of fish paste. Adjust heat so temperature does not climb. Put a baking sheet lined with a triple layer of paper towels near stovetop.

5. Garnish mounded toasts by gently pressing a coriander leaf on each piece and sprinkling carrot or ham and sesame seeds. Carefully drop toast pieces, one by one, fish side down, into oil, adding only as many as can float freely. Adjust heat to maintain a steady temperature. Fry until toasts float high on surface of oil and fish is cooked, about 4 minutes. When nearly done, ladle a bit of oil over bread sides to turn them golden. Return oil to 375°F between batches.

6. With a large mesh spoon, remove toasts and place, bread side down, on paper towels. Let drain and cool several minutes. Serve on a colorful platter or in a steamer basket with sprigs of fresh coriander.

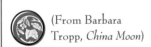 (From Barbara Tropp, *China Moon*)

Sautéed Chinese broccoli
Long-life noodles with crabmeat and mushroom
Sticky rice in lotus leaf
Fresh fruit

The Korean Noodle Banquet

The Korean banquet is much less elaborate and formal than the Chinese or the Japanese. The meal begins with a small cup of Korean sake, or *jung jong,* downed quickly like a shot. The courses are served all at the same time, the traditional low wooden table filling with dark mahogany or ceramic bowls, some larger, some smaller. The larger bowls contain the main dishes—soups, meats, vegetables, pancakes, and rice. The smaller bowls contain the condiments—several kinds of kimchi (some spicy, some salty, some soupy), dipping sauces, and chili sauce. In contrast to the food-in-the-middle style of Chinese banquets, each person has his or her own serving.

Korean meals must be a feast for the eyes. The presentation is important because all the food is laid out at once. Color is highlighted: the bright red spicy kimchi balancing with the cool white radish, deep green watercress atop translucent noodles. Cold and hot dishes, yin and yang, are balanced.

The wedding banquet is called *kook soo sang,* the "noodle banquet." It includes a variety of dishes to suit your taste and the season. The only must-have dish is the meal's namesake, a noodle soup called *kook soo.* Wheat noodles are boiled, then added to a clear beef broth. The more ambitious cooks will garnish the soup with vegetables such as fried zucchini or with tiny strips of fried egg. Here too noodles are a wish for a long and happy life.

Koreans also serve *dok,* a sticky rice cake similar to the Japanese *mochi.* It can come in a number of forms—sweetened, filled with bean paste, dotted with sesame seeds—and you'll see at least one kind at most festive meals. *Yakshik,* a sticky rice ball sweetened with brown sugar and dotted with chestnuts, jujubes, raisins, and pine nuts, is also popular. The nuts are a symbol for many children. Kimchi, the traditional vegetable pickle, also comes in a variety of ways: red, superhot cabbage; salted cabbage mixed with chestnuts, jujubes, shrimp, octopus; crunchy radish floating serenely in a cold sweet vinegar soup, to name but three. You'll find a variety of kimchi to sample at any Korean meal.

In larger American cities, you may find Korean restaurants that cater wedding parties and can provide *kook soo* or any other traditional dish you may desire. If you're planning a wedding banquet outside a restaurant, you may have problems finding a Western chef who can cook Korean foods. If you're determined to serve Korean food, ask if the wedding hall will let you carry in certain dishes. You might have the traditional *kook soo* at a smaller, family-only meal or at the rehearsal dinner.

Suggested Menus

TRADITIONAL
from Hangawi, New York City

Chap chae: Cold vermicelli with vegetables
Chun: Pancakes of fish or mung bean
Pyeon yook: Boiled sliced pork with prawn dipping sauce
Kalbee jim: Steamed barbecued short ribs
Dok: Rice cake
San chae: Nine mountain greens
Nok doo mook: Mung bean jelly with soy sauce
Shin sun lo: Empress steamboat with fish and meat
San jok: "Shish kabob" with meat and vegetables
Soo chung kwa: Cinnamon-sweet broth with persimmons

LOTUS SEED SOUP

This sweet soup, served in the middle of the wedding banquet, is a wish for sons.

½ *pound dried lotus seeds*
6 *cups water for steaming*
⅔ *cup sugar or rock candy*

1. Soak lotus seeds for 10 minutes in cold water. Drain and repeat procedure three times. Drain.
2. Take out green shoot from center of seeds, if necessary. (It's bitter.)
3. Steam lotus seeds over boiling water for 30 minutes. Remove to mixing bowl and add sugar. Mix until sugar dissolves, and serve in small bowls.

Note: Some dried lotus seeds contain baking soda and may be less brittle. Adjust soaking time accordingly.

 (From Diana Chow, Fullerton, California)

KOHAKU NAMASU (RED-AND-WHITE SALAD)

This beautiful salad is served at New Year's and other holidays because of its festive color. Serves four.

6 ounces daikon radish, peeled
1 medium carrot, peeled
2½ teaspoons salt
1 small piece dried konbu seaweed, wiped
Shreds lemon zest, soaked in cold water and squeezed dry

Amazu dressing:
6 tablespoons rice vinegar
6 tablespoons dashi (Japanese stock)
2 tablespoons sugar

1. Cut daikon and carrot into fine threads. Knead with salt and set aside for 30 minutes to soften.
2. Combine dressing ingredients in a small saucepan and bring just to boil to dissolve sugar, then set aside to cool.
3. Rinse daikon and carrot, and knead thoroughly until daikon is soft and translucent, squeezing out as much liquid as possible. Measure out 3 teaspoons dressing and

NOT-SO-TRADITIONAL
from Hangawi, New York City

VEGETARIAN

Chap chae: Cold vermicelli with vegetables
Dok: Rice cake
Chun: Pancakes of fish, mung bean, potato, or leek
Possam kimchi: Spicy pickled cabbage wrapped in whole cabbage
Shin sun lo: Steamboat soup with mushrooms, tofu, and vegetables
Koo kok pop: Nine kinds of rice with dates, mushrooms, and gingko nuts
Soo chung kwa: Cinnamon-sweet broth with persimmons
Kang chung: Cookie

Of late, I've grown very fond of wild geese. When I see one swimming or flying alone, I wonder where its mate is. You see, geese fly in pairs, one slightly in front of the other, so the goose behind can take advantage of the updraft created by the wings of the one in front. After a time, they switch places, allowing the one that was in front to rest a bit. Geese encourage each other, the one in back honking to the one in front. If one goose goes down because of sickness or gunshot, the other will fly to its side. There the goose will stay until its partner recovers or dies. And sadly, if the goose dies, its partner will never take another.

I wish for you the marriage of geese, full of devotion to each other, encouragement, loyalty, and everlasting love. *Kanpei!*

mix with vegetables; knead again and discard dressing that is pressed out.
4. Put vegetables in a clean bowl; pour in remaining dressing and mix well. Lay the *konbu* on top to give flavor; cover the bowl and refrigerate. The salad can be served after 30 minutes, but tastes better if left overnight. Remove the *konbu* to serve, and garnish with lemon zest.

(From Leslie Downer, *At the Japanese Table*)

Resource Guide

*It is impossible to name all the Asian-American businesses
that provide wedding services across the country. For a
complete listing of vendors in your area, contact your local
cultural center or Asian-American Chamber of Commerce.
Use this list to help you get started.*

CULTURAL CENTERS AND LIBRARIES

*To find out more about your culture's traditions, or to
do some digging into your own roots, visit a local cultural center or library. If you don't live near one, many
libraries will send or fax information upon request.*

ASIA SOCIETY
New York, NY
212-288-6400

ASIAN-AMERICAN CHAMBERS OF COMMERCE
Washington, DC
202-296-5221

ASIAN ART MUSEUM OF SAN FRANCISCO
San Francisco, CA
415-379-8800

THE METROPOLITAN MUSEUM OF ART
Costume Institute
New York, NY
212-650-2723

CHINESE
CHICAGO CHINATOWN
CHAMBER OF COMMERCE
Chicago, IL
312-326-5320

CHINESE CHAMBER OF COMMERCE
San Francisco, CA
415-982-3000

CHINESE CONSOLIDATED BENEVOLENT
ASSOCIATION OF NEW ENGLAND
Boston, MA
617-542-2574

CHINESE CULTURAL CENTER
Los Angeles, CA
213-626-7295

CHINESE CULTURAL CENTER
Houston, TX
713-789-4995

CHINESE HISTORICAL SOCIETY
OF SOUTHERN CALIFORNIA
Los Angeles, CA
213-621-3171

CHINESE INFORMATION AND CULTURE
CENTER, LIBRARY
New York, NY
212-373-1800

HOUSTON CHINESE CHAMBER OF COMMERCE
Houston, TX
713-498-4310

LOS ANGELES CHINESE
CHAMBER OF COMMERCE
Los Angeles, CA
213-617-0396

TAIPEI ECONOMIC AND CULTURAL OFFICE
Atlanta, GA
404-522-0481

TAIPEI ECONOMIC AND CULTURAL OFFICE
Chicago, IL
312-616-6716

TAIPEI ECONOMIC AND CULTURAL OFFICE
Boston, MA
617-737-2057

JAPANESE
CONSULATE OF JAPAN, INFORMATION CENTER
San Francisco, CA
415-777-3533

CONSULATE OF JAPAN,
CULTURAL INFORMATION CENTER
Chicago, IL
312-280-0400

CONSULATE OF JAPAN,
CULTURAL INFORMATION CENTER
New York, NY
212-371-8222

JAPAN AMERICA SOCIETY OF CHICAGO
Chicago, IL
312-263-3049

JAPANESE-AMERICAN CITIZENS' LEAGUE
Chicago, IL
312-728-7171

JAPANESE-AMERICAN CULTURAL &
COMMUNITY CENTER
Los Angeles, CA
213-628-2725

KOREAN

KOREAN-AMERICAN ASSOCIATION
Chicago, IL
312-878-1900

KOREAN ASSOCIATION OF NEW YORK
New York, NY
212-296-3221

KOREAN CULTURAL CENTER
Los Angeles, CA
213-936-7141

KOREAN CULTURAL SERVICE CENTER, LIBRARY
New York, NY
212-759-9550

KOREAN EMBASSY, INFORMATION CENTER
Washington, D.C.
202-939-5600

ASIAN-AMERICAN DESIGNERS

HAN FENG
New York, NY
212-695-9509

GEMMA KAHNG
New York, NY
212-398-6616

KANOJO
Irvine, CA
714-955-2250

YUMI KATSURA*
New York, NY
212-772-3760

HANAE MORI*
New York, NY
212-472-2352

VIVIENNE TAM
New York, NY
212-840-6470

VERA WANG*
New York, NY
212-628-3400

C. J. YOON ONO
New York, NY
212-274-1535

*Retail stores

Traditional Dress

Contact your local Asian-American Chamber of Commerce or cultural center for a list of dress shops in your area. Banquet halls, beauty shops, and photography studios also may rent traditional gowns.

Chinese

ANGIE'S BRIDAL
Angie Mycroft
Western and Asian dresses
Atlanta, GA
770-664-7057

HONG CHAN COMPANY
San Francisco, CA
415-362-5675

HYDRANGEA BRIDAL
Chicago, IL
708-323-9988

SALINA BRIDAL
Dress rental and photography
Flushing, NY
718-359-6699

Japanese

MARUKYO
Kimono rental, including wig, fan, and shoes
Los Angeles, CA
213-628-4369

MICHI BEAUTY SALON
Kimono rental, makeup, hair
Edgewater, NJ
201-941-1889
New York, NY
212-752-9229

TOKYO BRIDAL AND TUXEDO
Kimono rental, makeup, hair
Los Angeles, CA
213-617-3595

Korean

HOUSE OF WEDDINGS
Dress rental
Chicago, IL
312-463-2001

JI'S BOUTIQUE
Reston, VA
703-742-0577

NAKWON HANBOK
Flushing, NY
718-961-2507

PARIS BEAUTY SALON
Dress rental, makeup, hair
New York, NY
212-967-8282

WON-ANG WEDDING CENTER
Banquet hall, traditional gowns, beauty salon
Glen Burnie, MD
410-761-2630

G.YOUN BRIDAL AND TUXEDO CORPORATION
Flushing, NY
718-359-1187

JEWELRY

CULTURED PEARL ASSOCIATION
New York, NY
212-869-9162

MASON KAY JADE AND FINE JEWELRY
Denver, CO
800-722-7575

WEDDING RING ORIGINALS
New York, NY
212-751-3940

HENRY YAMADA JEWELERS
Specializes in family crests and hiragana *and* kanji
pendants; takes out-of-state orders
Little Tokyo, CA
213-613-0451

CHURCHES AND TEMPLES

BUDDHIST
BUDDHIST CHURCHES OF AMERICA—
JODO SHINSHU SECT
*There are sixty-one Buddhist churches throughout
the country.*
415-776-5600

VENICE HONGWANJI BUDDHIST TEMPLE
The Reverend George Matsubayashi
Culver City, CA
310-391-4351

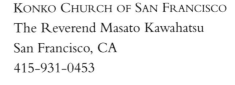

SHINTO

KONKO CHURCH OF LOS ANGELES
The Reverend Alfred Tsuyuki
The Reverend Tsuyuki travels extensively across the country for weddings.
Los Angeles, CA
213-268-6980

KONKO CHURCH OF SAN FRANCISCO
The Reverend Masato Kawahatsu
San Francisco, CA
415-931-0453

BAKERIES AND SWEET SHOPS

A stroll in your local Chinatown, Little Tokyo, or Little Korea will reveal bakeries or sweet shops, sometimes small and tucked away. There are also larger establishments, which often ship their delicacies anywhere in the country.

CHINESE

DIN HO BAKERY
Atlanta, GA
770-451-4608

GOLDEN CARRIAGE BAKERY
New York, NY
212-732-9898

KWONG WAH BAKERY
New York, NY
212-431-9575

PHOENIX BAKERY
The oldest bakery in L.A.'s Chinatown
Los Angeles, CA
213-628-4642 (Chinatown)
213-225-3791 (Lincoln Heights)

JAPANESE

FUGETSU-DO
Los Angeles, CA
213-625-8595

MONT BLANC
European pastries with a Japanese touch
Chicago, IL
847-228-5306

TORAYA
Ships orders anywhere in the United States
New York, NY
212-861-1700

KOREAN

JIN GO GAE
Flushing, NY
718-762-0655

NEW YORK BAKERY
Chicago, IL
312-604-8820

OH BOK BAKERY
Palisades Park, NJ
201-592-0152

CATERERS

CLASSIC CATERING
Asian foods
Los Angeles, CA
213-723-2438

FLOWERS

*If you are interested in Oriental-style arrangements
and can't find an Asian-American flower shop,
bring a picture to your florist and see what he or
she can do.*

CAMEO PRODUCTIONS
Catherine Matsumoto
Los Angeles, CA
619-792-0698

HIBIYA-KADAN USA
The only U.S. branch of the oldest Japanese florist
Los Angeles, CA
800-844-2492 or 310-225-3363

MIHO KOSUDA
New York, NY
212-922-9122

MAHALO FLOWERS
Specializes in Hawaiian leis
Los Angeles, CA
310-836-0439

YOKO MILLER
Hana To Yoko
Chicago, IL
312-822-9595

TOM UYENO
Toyo Griffith Park Florist
Los Angeles, CA
213-465-0514

MIRAGE FLORAL DESIGNS
Merle Kawai-Ahn
Diamond Bar, CA
909-861-7228

WHITE GARDEN FLORIST
Atlanta, GA
770-840-7177

PHOTOGRAPHERS/VIDEOGRAPHERS

Asian-American photographers and videographers come with the added benefit of knowing what's important to shoot during cultural ceremonies. Be sure to brief your photographer before the ceremony.

PHOTOGRAPHERS
JOEY IKEMOTO PHOTOGRAPHY
Torrance, CA
310-212-7366

JUNG HYUN LEE
Chicago, IL
312-989-0134

ALAN MIYATAKE
Toyo Miyatake Studio
San Gabriel, CA
818-289-5674

STUDIO NEW YORK ONE
Flushing, New York
718-353-7333

PAUL YAMASHIRO
Chicago, IL
312-883-0440

VIDEOGRAPHERS
RICK TAMASHIRO
Specializes in reception video presentations
Gardena, CA
310-715-1045

MUSIC AND ENTERTAINMENT

If you can't find a musician to perform traditional pieces, you can always look into the wide variety of music imported to this country on compact discs or cassette tapes. A local cultural center may know of Asian-American musicians in your area. And since the pool of musicians performing on traditional instruments is quite small, a call to, say, a koto player in Los Angeles might turn up a koto player in New York.

CHINESE

CHINESE MUSIC ENSEMBLE OF NEW YORK
Instrumental
New York, NY
718-796-6106

THE IMMORTALS
Lion dance troupe
Los Angeles, CA
818-281-4478

JAPANESE

HIROMI HASHIBE
Koto
Los Angeles, CA
818-576-4448

KOKIN GUMI
Traditional music
Los Angeles, CA
818-446-4783

RALPH SAMUELSON
Shakuhachi
New York, NY
212-373-4300

KOREAN

HANNA PRODUCTION
Korean band
Towson, MD
410-558-0542

KOREA ENSEMBLE
Instrumental, song, dance
Englewood Cliffs, NJ
201-947-0670

INVITATIONS

Ethnic printers will often work with Western printers to produce multilingual invitations.

CHINESE

HO TAI PRINTING AND BOOK STORE
San Francisco, CA
415-421-4218

SALINA BRIDAL
Flushing, NY
718-359-6699

SUNSHINE PRINTING & STATIONERY
Los Angeles, CA
213-629-2706

TOYO PRINTING
Los Angeles, CA
213-626-8153

JAPANESE

ACCESS JAPAN
New York, NY
212-576-1460

BIZZY FORMS
Los Angeles, CA
310-479-1676

TOYO PRINTING
Los Angeles, CA
213-626-8153

KOREAN

OFFICIAL PRESS
New York, NY
212-244-5320

BOOKSTORES

CHINESE
WORLD JOURNAL BOOKSTORE
Atlanta, GA
770-451-4809
Brooklyn, NY
718-871-5000
Flushing, NY
718-445-2661
New York, NY
212-226-5131

JAPANESE
KINOKUNIYA
Costa Mesa, CA
714-434-9986
San Francisco, CA
415-567-7625
San Jose, CA
408-252-1300
Los Angeles, CA
213-687-4480

Edgewater, NJ
201-941-7580
New York, NY
212-765-7766
Seattle, WA
206-587-2477

KOREAN
KORYO BOOKS
1-800-538-6070
Doraville, GA
404-455-3222
Fort Lee, NJ
201-461-0008
New York, NY
212-564-1844

DONG A
Los Angeles, CA
213-382-7100

STATIONERY STORES

CHINESE
SUNSHINE PRINTING & STATIONERY
Los Angeles, CA
213-629-2706

JAPANESE
BEVERLY'S
Los Angeles, CA
213-687-0528

KINOKUNIYA
Costa Mesa, CA
714-434-9986
Los Angeles, CA
213-687-4480
San Francisco, CA
415-567-7625
San Jose, CA
408-252-1300

Edgewater, NJ
201-941-7580
New York, NY
212-765-7766
Seattle, WA
206-587-2477

SPECIAL ARTIFACTS

AMAY
Personalized fortune cookies
Los Angeles, CA
213-626-2713

BUNKA-DO
Large selection of accessories for the Japanese wedding, including san-san-kudo *cups and* noshigami, *paper used to wrap gifts*
Los Angeles, CA
213-625-1122

CALICO COUSINS
Gayle Goya and Kevin Oshiro
Custom 1,001 crane designs; party favors with an Asian flair
La Palma and Gardena, CA
714-995-2283

HOUSE OF WEDDINGS
P'ye-baek *foods*
Chicago, IL
312-463-2001

LET'S KNIT YARN SHOP
Saeko Oyama
Custom 1,001 crane designs; works with out-of-state clients
Gardena, CA
310-327-4514

SUNSHINE PRINTING & STATIONERY
Chinese banners and wedding accessories
Los Angeles, CA
213-629-2706

GLEN AND ALAN TAO
1,001 crane displays
Walnut, CA
909-869-7759

SPECIAL STORES AND GIFT REGISTRIES

CHINESE PORCELAIN COMPANY
Asian ceramics
New York, NY
212-838-7744

FELISSIMO
Unique objects
New York, NY
212-247-7474
212-247-5656, ext. 135 or 136 for bridal
registry

NONG HYUP
Korean handicrafts and gourmet foods
Fort Lee, NJ
201-585-0700

RAFU BUSSAN
Imported Japanese goods, crystal, and kitchenware;
has a bridal registry
Los Angeles, CA
213-614-1181

TAKASHIMAYA
Select accessories and gifts reflecting East and West
New York, NY
800-753-2038

YAOHAN
Food, clothing, electronics
Los Angeles, CA
213-687-6699
Chicago, IL
847-956-6699
Edgewater, NJ
201-941-9113

Newspapers

Local Asian-American papers—some printed in English—can be a good source of wedding services. Rafu Shimpo in L.A. offers an annual bridal guide. Some papers also print wedding announcements, although they may charge a fee.

Chinese

Asian Week
San Francisco, CA
415-397-0220

Chinese Times
San Francisco, CA
415-982-6206

World Journal
San Francisco, CA
415-692-9525

World Journal
Atlanta, GA
770-451-4509

World Journal
New York, NY
212-226-5131

Japanese

Chicago Shimpo
Chicago, IL
312-478-6170

Rafu Shimpo
Los Angeles, CA
213-629-2231

Yomiuri
New York, NY
212-765-1111

Korean

Central Daily News
New York, NY
718-361-7700

Korea Times
Los Angeles, CA
213-487-5323

Korea Times
New York, NY
718-784-4500

Korean Central Daily
Los Angeles, CA
213-389-2500

Wedding Planners

These consultants can be an invaluable help. The national Association of Bridal Consultants is becoming more aware of the special needs at ethnic weddings.

ASSOCIATION OF BRIDAL CONSULTANTS
New Milford, CT
This organization can provide the names of accredited wedding planners in your area.
203-355-0464

CATHERINE MATSUMOTO
Wedding specialist
Delmar Hilton
Delmar, CA
619-792-5200

LOIS PEARCE
Beautiful Occasions
Ms. Pearce is director of ethnic diversity at the Association of Bridal Consultants.
203-248-2661

Books

Yosano Akiko, *Tangled Hair: Love Poems of Yosano Akiko,* trans. Dennis Maloney and Hide Oshiro. White Pine Press

Patricia Buckley-Ebrey, *Inner Quarters: Marriage and the Lives of Chinese Women in the Sung Period.* University of California Press

Noh Chin-hwa, *Korean Traditional Cooking.* Hollym

Lesley Downer, *At the Japanese Table.* Chronicle Books

Walter Edwards, *Modern Japan Through Its Weddings.* Stanford University Press

Laurel Kendall, *Getting Married in Korea: Of Gender, Morality, and Modernity.* University of California Press

Wu-chi Liu and Irving Yucheng Lo, eds., *Sunflower Splendor.* Anchor/Doubleday

One Hundred Poems from One Hundred Poets. The Hokuseido Press

Carol Stepanchuk and Charles Wong, *Mooncakes and Hungry Ghosts: Festivals of China.* China Books & Periodicals

Barbara Tropp, *China Moon Cookbook.* Workman

C. A. S. Williams, *Outlines of Chinese Symbolism & Art Motives.* Dover

Norio Yamanaka, *The Book of Kimono: The Complete Guide to Style and Wear.* Kodansha International

Index

Credits and Permissions

Black-and-white illustrations

p. 4 From Carol Stepanchuk and Charles Wong, *Mooncakes and Hungry Ghosts: Festivals of China.* © 1991 Carol Stepanchuk and Charles Wong. Published by China Books and Periodicals, Inc., San Francisco.

p. 6 Anonymous (formerly attributed to Wang Juzheng), *Two Women with a Parakeet in a Garden.* Courtesy Museum of Fine Arts, Boston. Harriet Otis Fund.

p. 7 Illustration by Wendy K. Lee. From Carol Stepanchuk and Charles Wong, *Mooncakes and Hungry Ghosts: Festivals of China.* © 1991 Carol Stepanchuk and Charles Wong. Published by China Books and Periodicals, Inc., San Francisco. Reprinted by permission of Wendy K. Lee.

p. 8 Hishikawa Moronobu, *Lovers Seated on the Ground Beside a Clump of Flowering Plants.* The Metropolitan Museum of Art, Harris Brisbane Dick Fund, 1949 (JP 3069).

p. 9 Gourd-shaped ewer, with reeds and herons. The Metropolitan Museum of Art, Fletcher Fund, 1927 (27.119.2).

p. 10 Limb Hijoo, *kirogi* (wedding duck). From Robert Moes, *Auspicious Spirits: Korean Folk Paintings and Related Objects* (exhib. cat.). © 1983 International Exhibitions Foundation, Washington, D.C.

p. 17 From Northeast Drama Institute, People's Republic of China, ed., *Traditional Chinese Textile Designs.* © 1980 Dover Publications, Inc.

p. 19 Illustration by N. C. Wan.

p. 21 From W. M. Hawley, *Japanese Family Crests.* Courtesy W. M. Hawley Private Oriental Library.

p. 23 Yoshinobu, *The Goddess Benten Playing the Biwa.* Museum für Völkerkunde, Vienna. Photo archive no. 40.706.

p. 80   Ma Lin, album leaf: *Orchids.* The Metropolitan Museum of Art, Gift of The Dillon Fund, 1973 (1973.120.10). Photograph by Malcolm Varon.

p. 82   From Northeast Drama Institute, People's Republic of China, ed., *Traditional Chinese Textile Designs.* © 1980 Dover Publications, Inc.

p. 87   The Metropolitan Museum of Art, Bequest of Mary Stillman Harkness, 1950 (50.145.741).

p. 89   Kwon Ok-yun and Lee Byung-boc, *Peonies.* From Robert Moes, *Auspicious Spirits: Korean Folk Paintings and Related Objects* (exhib. cat.). © 1983 International Exhibitions Foundation, Washington, D.C.

p. 90   Courtesy Korean Overseas Information Service, Washington, D.C.

p. 93   From Valery M. Garrett, *Chinese Clothing: An Illustrated Guide.* © 1994 Valery M. Garrett. Published by Oxford University Press, Hong Kong.

p. 94   Museum für Völkerkunde, Vienna. Photo archive no. 36.792.

p. 95   Illustration by Wendy K. Lee. From Carol Stepanchuk and Charles Wong, *Mooncakes and Hungry Ghosts: Festivals of China.* © 1991 Carol Stepanchuk and Charles Wong. Published by China Books & Periodicals, Inc., San Francisco. Reprinted by permission of Wendy K. Lee.

p. 109   Artwork by Glen and Alan Tao, Walnut, California (909-869-7759).

p. 110   Kano Shoei, *Birds in a Landscape.* Courtesy Museum of Fine Arts, Boston. Fenollosa-Weld Collection.

p. 111   Diagram published originally by Heian International, Inc.; adapted by N. C. Wan.

p. 116   Photograph by Denise Dmochowski.

p. 127   Courtesy Toraya, New York.

p. 129   Ito Jakucho, *Phoenix and Sun.* Courtesy Museum of Fine Arts, Boston. William Sturgis Bigelow Collection.

p. 134   Chen Rong, *Nine Dragon Scroll.* Courtesy Museum of Fine Arts, Boston. Francis Gardner Curtis Fund.

p. 1   Kitagawa Utamaro, *Three Contemporary Beauties.* Courtesy Museum of Fine Arts, Boston. Spaulding Collection.

p. 1   Attributed to Emperor Huizong, *Court Ladies Preparing Newly Woven Silk.* Courtesy Museum of Fine Arts, Boston. Chinese and Japanese Special Fund.

p. 2   Panels from a wedding robe: two cranes (left) and single phoenix (right). Courtesy Board of Trustees of the Victoria & Albert Museum.

p. 3   National Palace Museum, Taipei, Taiwan, Republic of China.

p. 4   Top left: Makeup by Aiko Yamano. Photograph courtesy Jane A. Yamano.

p. 4   Top right: Asian Art Museum of San Francisco, The Avery Brundage Collection (B85 M16). Photograph © 1991 Asian Art Museum of San Francisco. All rights reserved.

p. 4   Bottom: Courtesy Board of Trustees of the Victoria & Albert Museum.

p. 5   Top left: Courtesy Korean Overseas Information Service, Washington, D.C.

p. 5   Top right: Courtesy Taiwan Museum.

p. 5   Bottom: Asian Art Museum of San Francisco, The Avery Brundage Collection (1995.54). Photograph © 1996 Asian Art Museum of San Francisco. All rights reserved.

p. 6   Top: Bride's and groom's attire designed by Yumi Katsura.

p. 6   Bottom: Photograph by Joey Ikemoto, Torrance, California (310-212-7366).

p. 7   Top: Bride's dress by Lazaro, gloves by Finale, shoes by Stuart Weitzman, flowers by Sura Kayla; bridesmaid's dress by Judd Waddell for Jim Hjelm, shoes by Yves Saint Laurent. All jewelry by Cultured Pearl Association. As seen in *Bride's* magazine. Photograph © Jean Noel L'Hammeroult.

p. 7   Bottom: Flowers by Miho Kosuda. As seen in *Bride's* magazine. Photograph © Richard Pierce.

p. 8   Top: Dress designed by Yumi Katsura.

p. 8   Bottom: Bride's dress by Ulla-Maija Atelier, earrings by Cultured Pearl Association, flowers by Miho Kosuda. As seen in *Bride's* magazine. Photograph © Jean Noel L'Hammeroult.

Prose and verse

p. 3   "The outside grandparents." Maxine Hong Kingston, *China Men.* © 1980 Maxine Heng Kingston. Published by Alfred A. Knopf.

p. 7   "Distant and faint." Anonymous, from Wu-chi Liu and Irving Yucheng Lo, eds., *Sunflower Splendor.* Poem trans. Dell R. Hales. © 1975 Wu-chi Liu and Irving Yucheng Lo. Reprinted by permission of Dell R. Hales.

p. 8   "Lying with my lover." Yosano Akiko, from *Tangled Hair: Love Poems of Yosano Akiko,* trans. Dennis Maloney and Hide Oshiro. © 1987 Dennis Maloney and Hide Oshiro. Reprinted by permission of White Pine Press, 10 Village Square, Fredonia, NY 14063.

p. 15   "When I first met." Kim Wookyu, from *Classical Korean Poems (Sijo);* ed. Kim Unsong. © 1987 One Mind Press. Reprinted by permission of Kim Unsong/ One Mind Press.

p. 16   "Come make one heart." Han Yong-Woon, from *Meditations of the Lover,* trans. Yonghill Kang and F. Keely. Published by Yonsei University Press, Seoul, 1970. Reprinted by permission of Yonsei University Press.

p. 22   "Kwan-kwan." From Mrs. J. G. Cormack, *Chinese Birthday, Wedding, Funeral, and Other Customs.* © 1923 Mrs. J. G. Cormack. Published by and reprinted by permission of The Commercial Press, Beijing Branch Works.

p. 46   "May my dream." Park Hyokwan, from *Classical Korean Poems (Sijo),* ed. Kim Unsong. © 1987 One Mind Press. Reprinted by permission of Kim Unsong / One Mind Press.

p. 48   "On her third to the last evening." From Maxine Hong Kingston, *China Men.* © 1980 Maxine Hong Kingston. Published by Alfred A. Knopf.

p. 53   "Without speaking." Yosano Akiko, from *Tangled Hair: Love Poems of Yosano Akiko*, trans. Dennis Maloney and Hide Oshiro. © 1987 Dennis Maloney and Hide Oshiro. Reprinted by permission of White Pine Press, 10 Village Square, Fredonia, NY 14063.

p. 69   "On the hilltop." From Vera Lee, *Something Old, Something New.* © 1994 Vera Lee. Published by Sourcebooks, Inc.

p. 85   "Before I came." Fujiwara-no Yoshitaka, from *One Hundred Poems from One Hundred Poets*. Waka translation © 1956 Heihachiro Honda. Published by the Hokuseido Press.

p. 88   "The peach tree." From Mrs. J. G. Cormack, *Chinese Birthday, Wedding, Funeral, and Other Customs.* © 1923 Mrs. J. G. Cormack. Published by and reprinted by permission of The Commercial Press, Beijing Branch Works.

p. 99   "May the bride bow." From Patricia Buckley-Ebrey, *Inner Quarters: Marriage and the Lives of Chinese Women in the Sung Period.* © 1993 The Regents of the University of California. Published by the University of California Press.

p. 105   "At Katushika." From Vera Lee, *Something Old, Something New.* © 1994 Vera Lee. Published by Sourcebooks, Inc.

p. 106   "The mandarin ducks." From Patricia Buckley-Ebrey, *Inner Quarters: Marriage and the Lives of Chinese Women in the Sung Period.* © 1993 The Regents of the University of California. Published by the University of California Press.

p. 107   "Soaking with flowing tears." Kiyowara-no Motosuke, from *One Hundred Poems from One Hundred Poets*. Waka translation © 1956 Heihachiro Honda. Published by The Hokuseido Press.

p. 120   Recipe for *possam kimchi* from Noh Chin-hwa, *Traditional Korean Cooking.* © 1985 Hollym Corporation, Publishers.

p. 129   Recipe for *soo chung kwa* from Noh Chin-hwa, *Traditional Korean Cooking.* © 1985 Hollym Corporation, Publishers.

p. 130   Recipe for Spicy Fish Toasts from Barbara Tropp, *China Moon Cookbook.* © 1992 Barbara Tropp. Reprinted by permission of Workman Publishing Company, Inc. All rights reserved.

p. 134   Recipe for *kohaku namasu* from Lesley Downer, *At the Japanese Table: New and Traditional Recipes.* © 1993 Lesley Downer. Published by Chronicle Books, San Francisco.